Love is
a time of enchantment:
in it all days are fair and all fields
green. Youth is blest by it,
old age made benign: the eyes of love see
roses blooming in December,
and sunshine through rain. Verily
is the time of true-love
a time of enchantment—and
Oh! how eager is woman
to be bewitched!

THE WICKED WYNSLEYS

Mab and her young actor bought the mansion as their future home. Until the marriage she would live there with her sister. But soon her house of hopes is smashed and she finds herself, her sister, and her future husband actors on a stage of death.

Books by Alanna Knight
in the Ulverscroft Large Print Series:

A STRANGER CAME BY
THE WICKED WYNSLEYS

ALANNA KNIGHT

THE WICKED WYNSLEYS

Complete and Unabridged

ULVERSCROFT
Leicester

First Large Print Edition
published February 1990

British Library CIP Data

Knight, Alanna
 The wicked Wynsleys.—Large print ed.—
Ulverscroft large print series: romance, suspense
I. Title
823'.914[F]

ISBN 0-7089-2139-6

Published by
F. A. Thorpe (Publishing) Ltd.
Anstey, Leicestershire
Set by Rowland Phototypesetting Ltd.
Bury St. Edmunds, Suffolk
Printed and bound in Great Britain by
T. J. Press (Padstow) Ltd., Padstow, Cornwall

1

THIS was an alien land and I was the first woman born. In this lonely kingdom haunted by wild geese and curlews who remembered that once, long ago, it had belonged to the sea, I had been allowed the privilege of watching the world's dawn. The shimmering of silver light across the fens, the sunlight and thunder spears of rainclouds and Noah's rainbow, all gaining momentary supremacy in a landscape flung like a crumpled counterpane across whale-backed hills and wooded valleys—

The car's brakes, violent and agonized, cut across my dream—

"Are you sure this is the right road?" asked Derek.

It wasn't, and to cut a long story short, if I hadn't been a chronic navigator, my map-reading bedevilled by day-dreams, we would have missed Wynsley Manor completely. Through all that was left of the village of Wynsley and out onto the motorway, I would never have discovered my beloved country. To one born and bred on the wild Scottish borders, East Anglia was more alien than the Swiss Alps or the isles of Greece. I had never got over the remarkable fact that south of the Humber I felt as if I should have a passport and I remained surprised and gratified that the people spoke a language I could understand—mostly. It was intriguing, this common tongue, for in every other way I felt different. Yet once, generations back, an ancestress of mine had been brought back from this area by a seafaring Fenwick, to die among the wild Border hills. Of consumption, they said, but when I came to know this dear land, I thought it more likely to have been of longing.

"This can't be right, Mab."

We were advancing into a maze of hedgerows, from which bindweed stretched out like beseeching hands and clutched at the car. A naturalist's paradise unspoilt disappeared under our wheels with every hedge flower known to man—I glimpsed the familiar ones—bluebell, cow parsley, tall buttercups. The car moaned and swayed and protested like an overwrought prima donna. This was no place for a well-kept, deeply cherished Porsche Carrera. Tansy mingled with the heady perfume of orange blossom drifted in through the open windows.

"Oh, Derek—smell that. Divine!"

Derek paused, sniffed the air as if it might give indication of direction, and promptly began to sneeze. I had forgotten that he was plagued with hay fever. A walk or drive through a country lane with a high pollen count at midsummer was not an adventure to be undertaken lightly.

"I can't smell a thing," said Derek thickly. "Dammit—" The car had encountered a large stone and shuddered to a quivering stop, its beautiful lines resentfully all a-tremble. "For God's sake, Mab, this can't be the road through Wynsley."

"Of course it can—it's just a dot on the map." But I wasn't sure. Uneasiness and guilt were creeping over me. Sharp left or was it a second left? Strange that after all these years I still recall that moment with a shiver of fear. Sharp left or second left? Intention, accident, the celestial toss of a coin?

"I expect you were taking a nap again."

"I wasn't sleeping—I was watching the road."

"Liar—I've seen you dreaming with your eyes wide open. Give me the map." Derek took out his reading glasses with the furtive movement that indicated his pride loathed such a necessity. It was an action I associated with smart cafés rather than lonely lanes, where one of his adoring fans might learn—and whisper it abroad—that Sir Amyas Symon wore specs off the telly. My flicker of amusement was tinged with pity that male vanity could condemn him to live so uncomfortably in a half-dim world, with an allergy to contact lenses.

"You've done it again, Mab," he yelled. "*That*'s the road we want—*not* this one—" He cut short my apologies. "How in heaven's name am I ever going to get turned in this wilderness?"

Trying to look contrite, which I was, and busy and efficient, which I wasn't, I opened the door and stared out into the lane, an action which set a covey of nesting birds screeching heavenward beyond the jungly hedgerow. A sound of marching—feet—no, hooves. There were cows approaching.

4

"Shall I get out and go ahead? I'll be pathfinder," I added, not very enthusiastically.

Derek seized my arm. "Pathfinder? Please, God, no—that'll mean carrying you off to casualty in the nearest hospital with a broken leg, if I know you. Just stay where you are and we'll press on until I find somewhere to turn."

Pressing on was a rather apt description as we moved up the lane yard by yard with Derek cursing while I heaped apologies upon his curses.

"A fine short cut! We'll be lucky if we're out of here by midnight."

He was in no mood to be reminded that the short cut had been his idea. In theory it would cut off fifteen miles and get us on to the motorway to Derbyshire, where the next *Adventure of Amyas* was on location. Sir Amyas Symon, Queen's Adventurer, the Queen being Bess and Amyas a kind of sixteenth-century James Bond, complete with luscious girls with bosoms bursting out of farthingales instead of bikinis. The villainy was unbelievable and although the critics gave it a terrible rousting, millions of love-starved housewives all over Britain turned on their telly just after the news three times a week to see how Sir Amyas escaped from the latest fiend. And the fan mail for Derek Wynsley—real name Bill Brown—piled high on the studio's reception desk. He never answered it. Occasionally a secretary with time on her hands made a darting incursion into it, acknowledging receipt and saying "thank you." Which was where I came into Derek's life—

The car edged forward with great grindings and lurchings, the engine whimpered, coughed and was silent.

"Ye gods, Sir Amyas, I fear the beast is mortal wounded!"

"Bloody hell, that's a spring gone. And you know what you can do with your Amyas witticisms," he added with an illustrative gesture.

I offered to go on foot and explore, unarmed, the prospect before us, resisting a quip about a long lane that has no turning from Episode 6: "The Spanish Spy." It was not at all well-received, and leaving him with his head under the bonnet of the car, swearing with an admirable fluency which would have shocked his more genteel fans, I trudged up through the nettles and wilderness, dashing aside briars and brambles and prickly bushes. I screamed as something brushed against my ankle.

"Are you all right?" shouted Derek.

I did a quick inspection. "I think I encountered an adder."

"Try not to, darling. They're poisonous."

"It was warm."

"Oh, you're all right then. Adders are cold," he added cheerfully. "Be with you in a minute—"

"I'd be grateful. Crawling through the briars to the Sleeping Beauty's castle is man's work—"

And at that moment, like the answer to a prayer, the lane twisted, thinned out and widened into a track patterned by the heavy wheels of farm machinery. And I found myself face to face with a large and handsome black cat, balancing its way daintily along a wooden fence which led into an apple orchard. He was used to visitors and came to meet me full of dazzling feline charm and wheedling purrs as if to remind me of his human counterpart, the effusive lady at the cocktail party with whom I was rather too familiar. As I stroked that sleek head, the face seemed to smile, reminding me that this was witch country.

This great tawny landscape before me had seen the birth of the greatness of England. The Romans had coveted it, the names familiar to every schoolchild had once been its children—Hereward the Wake, Cardinal Wolsey, Horatio Nelson. A great queen Boadicea rode out in her chariot against the invaders, proving that woman's liberation was no twentieth-century invention. There were other queens too who had called it home. Mary Tudor before she earned the epithet of "Bloody Mary" lived here as a girl playing with her dollies. Her mother, ill-fated Catherine of Aragon, died here of cancer, neglected by Henry the Eighth, who feared above all things death and disease. In this country Catherine's rival child, who was to be Elizabeth of England, hunted, riding like a man, her red hair flying. It was a land of men, too. Powerful, rich and ruthless men, made wealthy from the wool trade. In its great forests kings had dawdled with their lights o'love while on the lookout for better game, the huge deer herds. After those early eager rapists the Vikings, Normans and Angles, it had been distantly threatened by Napoleon, and in living memory, by Hitler.

The cat, disappointed at my neglect, moved reproachfully away towards a gate. I followed, and among the rich smells of hawthorn and the blackbird's warning cry, I saw a house. A house of rose-red brick, with tall twisted chimneys and the sun touching mullioned windows with an illusion of welcome. Totally unexpected and totally beautiful, it waited, a jewel in a setting whose perfection argued against its creator being man.

In one of the many upper windows, something moved. A pale head, too distant to be clearly male or female, leaned out, looked across the wooded valley, and closed the window again. I turned.

Derek had reached my side and we gazed wordlessly across at the house. He whistled: "What a beauty! Doesn't look as if anyone lives there."

"Someone does. Up at the window there —I saw them close it."

"Great," said Derek. "Then the chances are that there is a phone and I can get hold of a garage—we'll have to be towed back to the road."

Weeds ranged almost to the front door. Within a few feet they stopped, cleared from a modern pebbled path with a sundial resting quietly upon it. We had ample opportunity to consider the passage of time, since no one came to answer the old-fashioned bell, which seemed to resound not only through the house but through the entire district.

"Must be deaf as a post," said Derek, moving back to stare up at the windows. "Are you sure you saw someone, Mab? It looks empty to me. There's no smoke from the chimneys, either," he added with a man's typical indifference to the fact that this was a warm summer's day.

"Let's go," I whispered. The thought of someone sitting upstairs listening to the bell and not answering the door filled me with a strange unease. There had to be very good reason for that noise being ignored. Most householders are curious enough to want to know who is outside. When I said so, Derek, exploring the tangle of weeds which had once constituted the main drive, laughed.

"Good reason—don't be daft. Ah," he held up a board in triumph. "Here's your good reason, darling. Look what I've found."

It read: "Wynsley Manor. Vacant Possession. For Sale or Rent. Enquiries to H. Willis, High Street, Abchester." It was a very old board, and faded. The post which supported it was rotten.

I looked up at the windows. "I was sure—"

"Perhaps you saw a caretaker, having a quick look round—perhaps she'd gone before we arrived. Out the back way."

"He, you mean. I'm almost certain it was a man—with fair hair."

Derek shrugged. It was unimportant. "Now we're here, we might as well get a closer look."

We stared in at all the windows. It was too dark to see more than richly panelled rooms with latched doors, marks where carpets and furniture had reclined. Through an open door, a glimpse of a great oak staircase, or the foot of it, with a shaft of sunlight trapped like a stage spotlight, full of soft warm light and dust motes.

"It's beautiful." And we stood there holding hands, with idiot smiles of pleasure. Derek, assuming the role of Sir Amyas, went forward boldly and grappled hopefully with the handle of the great door which suggested original Tudor. Defeated momentarily, he went round and systematically tried all the lower windows. I followed at a respectful distance, prepared to take immediate flight as I had done in distant childhood, should the irate owner appear, his wrath to be reckoned with. I was secretly glad when Derek came to the ivy-clad stone wall whose stout door, also original, cut off the back of the house.

"What a place," said Derek.

"Indeed yes and what a setting for Sir Amyas," I said, and he grinned sheepishly.

"Great minds think alike, eh, Mab?" He rubbed his chin. "It does say Sale or Rent." He moved the board with his foot. "How about it, darling?"

"How about what?" I said cautiously, having been involved in rather too many of his mad schemes. I had made up my mind—this time it was marriage or nothing. And mostly it was nothing, although I didn't need Derek to remind me that many a woman more beautiful, talented and sweeter-natured than I would have given her crowned teeth to brag of a great emotional experience with Sir Amyas. In the manner of many lesser men who acquire greatness by having it thrust upon them, so had Derek acquired virtue. It didn't come naturally to him to behave with celibacy. He liked a romp in the hay —a lot of romps in the hay, as a matter of fact. Unluckily, his wife Liz had come upon him and, patience exhausted, had decided to make him pay dearly in the only way she knew how—alimony. There were more laughs in their elaborate cat-and-mouse arrangement of detectives spying upon each other than ever found their way into the *Adventures of Amyas.*

"And," as Derek woefully remarked, donning his dark glasses at frequent intervals, "there are still six months to pay before the divorce."

Now he was staring thoughtfully at the windows. "This place has possibilities. It's near enough to the studio to commute every day—or at least come home at week-ends. And I've always fancied living near town—" I groaned. I could see another madcap scheme clearly forming inside that handsome head. "Yes—and once we get married, I can come home every night—"

I thought I had misheard. "Would you mind repeating that, at dictation speed?"

He stopped looking at the house, and smiled at me instead. "Certainly. You can live here until the divorce comes through, get the place in order, ready for us getting married. You idiot, come here."

He kissed me, and my heart gave a lurch of happiness. I never failed to be amazed that Derek Wynsley really intended to marry his ordinary secretary Mab Fenwick. Now, as we traced our footsteps, I was with him all the way in his bout of enthusiasm. It wasn't often that the same idea struck us both at the same time—except for carnal ones, which weren't allowed at the moment. I thought of living in this lovely house, and even the fact that the car obstinately refused to start failed to depress Derek. Sir Amyas Symon, Queen's courtier, he saw himself in the perfect setting of Wynsley Manor—what publicity! How the press were going to love it!

"I'm sure the *Radio Times* will do a colour feature," he said. "And I'm about due for a *Telegraph* supplement—"

All that remained of Wynsley was a Saxon church with a lych-gate, a handsome Tudor inn, and in a half-hearted attempt to keep up with a present, a garage fiercely adorned with petrol signs and tempting offers of triple stamps.

The garage attendant came out of his handsome glass office and when Derek explained that the car was unavoidably absent due to being bogged down in the lane back there, the man received this news with ill-concealed mirth. He had never heard of anyone wanting to go up there, and he gave us, for good measure, a coy glance which made me colour with indignation of the righteous variety.

"Sounds as if we'll need to tow it back to the road, sir. Have to wait until morning, I'm afraid—I'm short-handed at the moment and you won't get any of the farm lads working after tea-time."

"Where's the nearest town?"

"Abchester, sir. Two miles away."

15

Derek groaned. "Any hope of a taxi?"

"No, sir, 'fraid not. But the Wynsley Arms across the road there will give you a room. They're fairly quiet mid-week."

Fairly quiet was something of an overstatement, but the Wynsley Arms were pleased to give us a room.

"No, two rooms please," said Derek fiercely, adding with old-fashioned disapproval, "This young lady is my fiancée."

When Derek signed the register, the shrug that indicated our domestic sleeping arrangements were no concern of theirs, changed into delighted interest.

"Ah, sir, I thought we had seen you somewhere—of course, on the telly. Fascinating that you should come to Wynsley. I expect you're related to the family," our host added with pride.

"Alas, no. It isn't my real name. However, my agent recommended it one day when we were driving through here— I'm glad I chose it. It's certainly brought me good luck."

"As I hope your stay in Wynsley will add to it, sir."

The manager, who looked as if he might be a source of helpful information on

16

Wynsley Manor, proved a disappointment. A retired policeman, he had bought the Arms because he was recommended quiet on account of his bad heart. However, he was disposed to be friendly. It wasn't—as he pointed out—every day that they got a famous television actor. From the depressed appearance of the place, it wasn't every day that they even had drinking customers.

"Things have changed since they built the motorway. All business amounts to is tourists who get lost and a few folk over from Abchester at the weekends."

"What about the Manor?"

"The Manor, sir?" He looked blank.

"Yes, the big house we saw down the lane back there."

"Oh, Wynsley—no one goes there these days, sir. Been derelict since—" he paused and stared at the ceiling, either thoughtful about dates or—I had a sudden impression that he was reluctant to continue. "A long time now, it's been empty," he added lamely.

"We found a notice board saying it was for sale or rent."

"No one would want to rent that place,

sir," he laughed. "As for sale—" he frowned. "I've never seen any notice board—where was it?"

"We found it lying on the ground."

"That explains it. Must have been lying for a long time. Last I heard about Wynsley was when the old lady died—" He bit his lip and would have liked to bite back the words, I was sure. The pause was so long that Derek said:

"You were saying?"

"Well, I only heard that it had become the property of some relative of hers who lived in America—or was it Australia. I can't remember exactly. Anyway, it's just been left to rot. There's been plenty of talk about extending the motorway—I expect there's some truth in it. They'll be bringing the bulldozers in on us yet—"

I felt gloom and despondency creeping over me as we sat at the bar with the anachronism of a tiny portable black and white screen and some depressing feature film on the world in peril from starvation, which did nothing to alleviate my feelings of guilt at having put in a substantial order for roast duckling with orange sauce, preceded by river salmon. Derek had already ordered an excellent vintage bottle of wine. I knew he felt the same, as we moved into our candlelit annex to consume the splendid meal set before us. We had both built our hopes up on the flimsiest glimpse of Wynsley Manor. And Derek, whose series was, quite frankly, a little jaded and needing a personality boost, had built up the role he was to play in his own mind, interpreting all its nuances as lord of the manor of Wynsley. He would play it to perfection, and the publicity would have been invaluable. Poor Derek. I could see him saying goodbye to that colour feature, too.

In the circumstances we both drank more wine than discretion dictated, with the result that I parted from my love at my bedroom door with considerable regret. Had it not been that the last customer to come in might well have been Liz's detective tracking us down—for Derek was ready to swear he had seen *that* car following us earlier—I think I would have happily laid down my virtue without a qualm.

"Place is full of strangers tonight," said the manager and at that news Derek fairly leapt into the air. We were being followed —and nothing would convince him. He refused even to set foot over my doorstep and deprived me of even a chaste good-night kiss, scuttling along to his own room where, I was sure, he locked the door behind him.

The bedroom was in keeping with the rest of the inn, lacking within the Tudor charms of its exterior, an exterior which had, in the words of architects, been some-what freely restored. The bedroom was modern and rather awful with twin beds, candlewick spreads, and a dressing-table meant for dwarfs, since I needed to get down on my knees in order to see my face. A wall-cupboard with sliding doors that didn't, so I eventually put all my clothes on the one hard and uncomfortable chair. However, when I fell asleep it was into a gratifying dream of a four-poster bed, curtained and voluptuous, with a great wood fire cracking cheerfully in a vast stone fireplace. I was not alone, there was a lover—but I was ashamed to remember, come morning, that it wasn't Derek Wynsley in whose arms I lay and whose embrace I enjoyed.

Considering what terrors the future held, I felt those dreams, tormented but harmless, might have benefited by a small visit from my guardian angel, to offer at least a hint of caution or a warning to innocents.

2

ABCHESTER was just a fraction closer to the twentieth century than Wynsley. Its one main street boasted a supermarket and a Woolworths, plus a sprawl of houses which, according to statistics, housed a population of three thousand. Whereas Wynsley had undoubted charm, Abchester had red-brick weariness.

Our visit to Mr. Willis promised to be brief. Staring over his glasses in wing-collar, flowing tie, and dusty black suit, he reclined against a writing desk straight out of Charles Dickens. There was one anachronism. At some fairly recent date, the quill pen had been ousted by the ballpoint. This innovation was still a novelty to its owner, who punctuated all remarks by clicking it noisily, much to the detriment of my nerves.

"House, sir? Absolutely nothing to offer in Wynsley—sorry, sir—" click—click, he interrupted Derek's opening speech.

Derek frowned. He was not used to inter-ruptions when he took the stage. To Sir Amyas, the insult would have been answerable by an exchange of cold steel at dawn.

"I think you are mistaken—if you consult your books, you will find you have at least one house—Wynsley Manor." Sir Amyas was in fine form.

"Wynsley Manor." Mr. Willis smiled at him pityingly. "Most unsuitable. However, if you care to leave particulars of your requirements we will let you know the moment something suitable turns up in this area." And so saying, he gathered together his papers, considered the pen and clicked it several times in a decisive note of polite dismissal.

"Am I to understand that Wynsley Manor is no longer on the market?"

I had a sinking feeling that we had been forestalled, the broken board overlooked. The present tenant was the fair head I had seen at the window. However, last night Derek had insisted that if the house was ripe for the surveyor's chop to be signed, sealed and delivered over to the motorway for extinction, nobody would have cared for that garden. And the panelling, yes—all the handsome interior fittings would have been removed. It was cared for.

Mr. Willis was staring at Derek, and I said: "We would like to rent it, if it's available."

"We might even put in an offer," Derek said quickly.

I expected Mr. Willis to laugh out loud at that, but he looked bewildered and embarrassed. "I had forgotten Wynsley. I do beg your pardon. I am afraid the conditions are a little tedious. The house was up for sale, but I am out of touch with my client, who is at present abroad on some expedition and cannot be reached." Rubbing his chin thoughtfully, he looked us over. "I suppose there would be no objection to renting until he returned—" The price he mentioned was so low, I was certain that he had made some mistake. "Perhaps you had better look over the property first. You can always change your minds."

Then he did a strangely human thing. He leaned over the desk and said, in a voice that could only be described as imploring: "I would really advise you to wait until something more suitable turns up." Flustered and distressed by this sudden confidence, he stood up, opened his mouth and closed it firmly again. "Really—I wouldn't—"

"Wouldn't what?" asked Derek.

But Mr. Willis' professional zeal won the day. "Nothing, sir. I'll get the key and show you round."

Waiting in the car outside, Derek echoed my thoughts. "I wonder what the old boy's up to? He seemed very reluctant, didn't he?"

Mr. Willis led the way driving past the lane and to the church where a narrow, unassuming but well-kept road led past the manse and on to the Manor. As we approached, I was conscious of my fast-beating heart. Had that first impression been false? Would the inside be a bitter let-down? And what was the reason for the solicitor's reluctance?

Suddenly we turned the corner, and the sun on the south-facing windows gleamed like a welcoming smile. Again I was aware of the jewel-like setting, but the inside fulfilled every promise made by the exterior. A square panelled hall with several doors, one leading into a drawing-room, again panelled but with a stone fireplace, another into a library. There were no books, but I was heartened at shelves stretching from ceiling to floor, and up two steps, a deep embrasured window with a padded sill looked down into the garden. The handsome carved ceilings with coats of arms also continued from the hall. One room to the right and less ornate than the others had been converted into a dining-kitchen and large pantry, and looked directly into the orchard and across to the fence where I had had my first vision of the house. I was glad I would work with a window which would always remind me that destiny had led us through a summer lane deep in hedgerows and rewarded us with this house which was—as far as I was concerned—already ours.

We followed Mr. Willis up a great oak staircase with stained glass windows and their ancient coats of arms: "In death undefeated." It seemed an excellent choice, I thought, as Derek translated the Latin inscription. There were four bedrooms, two of them panelled and containing four-poster beds. The other two, less pretentious but comfortable, contained heavy Victorian bedroom suites. All had small stone fireplaces. When I exclaimed with delight over the four-posters, Mr. Willis said: "They were built into the house, put in before the windows—that's why they have been undisturbed through the ages. The room was literally built around the bed."

A solemn thought dashed cold water over my dreams. Where were we to find furniture for all those empty rooms downstairs? And Mr. Willis seemed to read my thoughts. "The furniture for the downstairs rooms—pictures and the like—were removed when the house was to be empty for some time. They will, of course, be included in the rent." When we both said how grateful we were, Mr. Willis held up a hand. "Of course, the furniture isn't all belonging to the original house, but the late Miss Wynsley was a collector of antiques, and tried as best she could to furnish within the period."

He led the way into a cavernous and gloomy bathroom. "This was installed about a hundred years ago," he said. It contained a full-length mirror spotted with age and damp, and a prehistoric bath of enormous proportions, standing on those animal paws so beloved of the Victorians. Unfortunately some tenant lacking in imagination had painted it green and as the paint suppurated with age and deterioration, it suggested that one might take a quiet bath in the lower half of a disembowelled dinosaur.

"Thank heaven the kitchen is modern at least," I whispered to Derek.

We were walking along a windowed corridor which stretched the length of the house and ended by a carved door which opened in two halves and on its panels depicted the heads of its Elizabethan owners.

"Yes," said Mr. Willis, "that is Francis Wynsley and his wife, who built the house in 1576. Very handsome, very handsome indeed." As he began to walk back toward the stairs, he turned. "Have you any questions?"

I looked at the door. "Yes, I should like to see inside this room."

He looked at me pityingly. "I'm afraid there isn't a room there now—at least not one anybody would want to use. You see, what we have here now is just a fragment of the original manor house. It was built in the E-pattern with which the Elizabethan builders flattered their Queen. And we have seen only one-third of it. This," he pointed to the carved door, "was the Long Gallery, which stretched from the middle right across to the other end of the house, in which were the more ceremonial apartments. Unfortunately a fire destroyed two-thirds of the house in the eighteenth century and it was left almost derelict for many years."

I turned the handle, and nothing happened. "This room is kept locked," said Mr. Willis. "There's nothing much to see—as I told you," he nodded reproachfully.

"I would like to see inside, in any case. Do you have a key?"

I felt that the key was produced with some reluctance—and I understood the reason why. A carved ceiling, the handsomest in the house, a stone fireplace ending in a horrendous green distempered wall with a modern window, and outside it, a crude iron balcony. "Bit of a sham now, I'm afraid," said Mr. Willis, hurrying us out and relocking the door behind him.

Yet, it wasn't a sham to me. In that crippled room, pride lingered, a remembrance still of beauty indestructible, beyond maiming and mutilation. Call it pride of spirit, I thought. It wasn't until afterwards that I realised that rooms which have memories of times past, which carry a remembrance of their better days, are also rooms that men sometimes call haunted.

For the moment, we followed Mr. Willis into the garden, where he unlocked the door with its trailing ivy and we found ourselves in a neat vegetable garden. "The Vicar and his wife take care of it," we were told. I was glad of something to alleviate the shock since this part of the house was entirely modern red-brick, twentieth century surburbia in its conception, even to the window and balcony in the locked room. There were no other windows facing this way, but the sight of a built-on garage drew a sigh of relief from Derek. "We'll take it," he said.

I went into the kitchen at Mr. Willis' request to see if there was any extra piece of equipment I might require which possibly was not in store. And, it was as I stood by the sink, searching the drawers for cutlery and kitchen knives, that I looked out of the window and saw a man on a black horse riding swiftly past the orchard. A fair head, pale as moonlight, a black cloak billowing on his shoulders—

Derek came in and I said: "Look, quickly—I swear that's the same man who was at the upstairs window last night—"

"Where—where?" said Derek peering past me.

"Over there, on horseback."

"I can't see anyone, Mab," he said irritably. "Are you sure?"

"Of course I'm sure. Oh, Derek, put your glasses on."

He extracted them from his pocket with a reproachful glare and I appealed to Mr. Willis, who was staring out of the window over my shoulder. "I'm almost certain that's the same man I saw closing the upstairs window last night. Do you see him?"

Mr. Willis shook his head. "I'm sorry, I don't see anyone. But then, I'm very short-sighted, too."

Derek moved us aside, staring out across the orchard. "Where is he?"

"Probably miles away by now. I thought he was the caretaker when I saw him before," I told Mr. Willis.

"Oh, I think you're mistaken. The house is kept locked, and I have the only keys. There is no caretaker."

He turned to Derek, rather sharply, I thought. "Did you see this man too, sir?"

"Of course he didn't. By the time he'd found his glasses, the man had gone—inside, we thought—because then we went over and knocked on the door, rang the bell—tried to get help, since our car had broken down."

Mr. Willis laughed soundlessly. "I presume you got no reply." He bit his lip. "Er—what was he like, this man?"

"I only saw his head. Thick straight hair, either very blond or grey—no, I'm certain it was blond, because I got the impression he was young."

"I will certainly make enquiries," promised Mr. Willis. However, as we followed him into the drawing-room again, I had the distinct impression that somehow my description of the "caretaker" had upset him.

"How much would the present owner be willing to accept—supposing we decided to buy?" asked Derek casually.

The sum mentioned made us blink. We couldn't have heard right. We exchanged bewildered glances. Why, one paid more for a suburban semi twenty miles from London.

"That's very—reasonable," gulped Derek, his aplomb failing him.

"Well, sir, as I told you, the owner lives abroad, and it is something of a white elephant."

Derek thought for a moment and remembered the motorway.

"Oh, the motorway," said Mr. Willis. "There was talk a year or two back, but they decided on the more direct route and took it straight over what used to be Shrivham Common instead. You need have no fears on that score."

"Oh, that's a relief." I asked about amenities and found there were buses to Abchester and that the Wynsley Arms was very accommodating about accepting deliveries from grocery vans and the like.

"Now, to whom do I make out the tenancy agreement. Mr. Fenwick, isn't it?"

"Oh, no—Miss Mirabel Fenwick. The tenancy is to be in my name."

Mr. Willis was clearly put out. He pursed his lips. "I beg your pardon—I had presumed I was dealing with a married couple. I'm afraid it would be most unsuitable for a young lady to live here on her own—so isolated, it could be—" he left it unsaid.

"We'll think of something," said Derek cheerfully. "As a matter of fact, we are thinking of getting married one of these days."

Mr. Willis shook his head. Our approaching marriage did nothing to set his mind or his morals at rest. His countenance grew more and more gloomy as we followed him outside, and I began to fear that he was changing his mind about our being suitable tenants. He turned and studied the upstairs windows thoughtfully.

"Which window was it—where you thought you saw someone?"

"That one—yes, the one you're looking at."

Mr. Willis averted his eyes hastily. "Impossible," he said.

"Perhaps we have a ghost," said Derek happily. Ghosts were always good for publicity. A haunted Elizabethan mansion would do Sir Amyas's image a power of good. A ghost would definitely merit the colour supplement.

"Absurd," said Mr. Willis, and we promised to call in and sign the agreement after lunch, which he recommended we take at the Wynsley Arms, declining politely our invitation to join us by patting his stomach delicately and rolling his eyes heavenward.

"What on earth was he so worried about?" I asked Derek as the car drove off.

"Indigestion, I expect."

"I mean about the house, stupid."

"I didn't think he was worried—relieved would be more like it—after all, he's got an unexpected tenant."

"You didn't get the impression that the man I saw last night somehow—frightened him?"

"Frightened him? Good grief, Mab, there you go with your fantasies again."

"I thought he seemed reluctant that I should stay there alone."

"Perhaps he thought you were going to set up a disorderly house." He studied me, laughing. "Come to think of it, no one—not even Mr. Willis—could imagine you in that particular role. You look too sweet and innocent—the Victorian maiden in distress. That's it," he added triumphantly. "I'll bet he has a daughter at home just like you, with honey-coloured hair and sea-green eyes."

"Idiot."

In the Wynsley Arms we were welcomed back like old customers and the counter was well wiped and polished before our drinks were set upon it. My host, avid with understandable curiosity about what had brought us back so soon, was disposed to be chatty until a phone call took him into the back premises.

Watching him disappear, Derek stared into his whisky and asked casually: "When exactly do you come into your little nest-egg, Mab? This summer some time, isn't it?"

I eyed him sternly. He knew damn well it was this summer, for all that manner of elaborate forgetfulness. It didn't fool me and Derek Wynsley was too good an actor to overlook one of the main cues in his forthcoming second venture into matrimony. Namely, my nest-egg, as he jokingly referred to it. After all, we both had long memories, and he knew and I knew that it had been part of the proposal in the cocktail bar at the Savoy at the end of a glittering television wedding party. Realising he was still sober and in his right mind, I said yes hastily, and he had laughed: "Drink up, my darling, here's to us. You're in a state of shock, and I'm only here for the nest-egg, remember."

This particular nest-egg was a handsome twenty thousand pounds which I was due to inherit under my grandmother's will on my twenty-fifth birthday. At twenty-five, Grandmother had imagined, my circumstances would be similar to her own at a quarter-century. She was by then a devoted wife and somewhat harassed mother of seven children. She fondly imagined that no young lady of even tolerable looks and education could remain on the shelf until such an age and that her only granddaughter would have reached the years of discretion. Dear Grandmother, may she rest in paradise where she belongs, for she had been barking up the wrong branch of the family tree. Ladies were ladies in her time, born and bred—and they stayed that way, while divorced men were only after one thing—and usually got it.

"I was thinking," said Derek. "Your birthday will be about the right time for the divorce—and our wedding. We could buy Wynsley—in your name, of course."

I heard myself agreeing enthusiastically. It was the mention of that wedding, that fairy-tale happy ending, that did it.

Mr. Willis promised to try to locate the owner, and shook his head over our folly. We shook hands all round and parted on cordial terms, but Derek was strangely silent as we drove back on to the motorway, making for London where I would pack up all my possessions, since we were moving to Wynsley next week. I wondered how my cousin Cora, with whom I shared the flat, would take the news.

"I was thinking about the divorce," said Derek. I should have guessed that. Any thoughts about Liz threw a considerable gloom over his natural ebullience. "You know, Mab, if Liz gets a whisper about the house at Wynsley before the divorce, that'll shoot my alimony into the five-figure class. She'll never believe for a moment that I'm innocently commuting." He paused while the main stream of the motorway tore past us and negotiated his way into the fast lane. "What about Cora?"

"Cora?" I asked sharply. His profile gave nothing away.

"Yes, Cora—she's going to need a new flat-mate when you leave. She won't be easy to please—I mean, all girls aren't as pleasant to live with as you are." He let that sink in but I refused to be provoked, since I could see exactly what he had in mind. "You know how wild she is about antiques and so forth. I'm sure she would be thrilled to share Wynsley—be chaperone, in fact—and I can always take her into town and back with me. Or there's the railway station at Abchester—"

"I don't want a chaperone," I said flatly. There are chaperones and chaperones. I just didn't want my twenty-year-old cousin who fancied Derek more than in the way of prospective kinship. Derek, poor dear, seemed oblivious of her attentions, which I considered painfully unsubtle.

"Oh, Mab, I know what you're thinking, but it just isn't true. It's your imagination again. She doesn't appeal to me." He grinned. "After all, it's the cousin with all the cash I'm interested in—"

That hurt—the unkindest cut of all—remembering his badly acted overtures about the nest-egg, I scowled until we left the motorway and stopped for petrol. Switching off, he put his arm around my shoulders. "You are a silly girl, being jealous. Do you think I'm that daft, not to know quality when I see it. Dear Cora has quantity, but those striking curves are a bit obvious to my taste."

I was remembering how, when we had first met Cora, dazzling, blonde and beautiful as a thirties movie queen, she drawled at him from the depths of the sofa: "Don't mind me, make yourself at home. I'm just the poor country cousin." Later, when Derek hinted that we would like a little time alone, she said: "All right,

I can take it—I know when I'm not wanted. I'm on to you, Mr. Derek Wynsley. It's just her money you're after. But chum, watch out, because if she ever slips on a banana skin or someone greases the stairs, the money'll all be mine."

Dear Cora. She was an idiot, and most of the time, when Derek wasn't around, I was fond of her. All our lives, being the only two female cousins, there had been a kind of rivalry between us. Begun, alas, before Cora was born, since Grandmother died that year. For some reason Cora's mother was incensed that the money was not to be shared between us, although it was my mother who had nursed Grandmother during the last trying years when even I could remember the shrill querulous old woman and Mother frequently in tears. She refused to let her go to a hospital and stuck by her to the end. Meanwhile Aunt Helen, Cora's mother, hardly ever put her nose in the door. She had married well and had social obligations. Mother, according to the family, had married beneath her, but she had obligations to those she had loved in better

41

days, which Aunt Helen conveniently forgot all about.

Old family wounds still rankled, and although Mother was all for sharing the "nest-egg," Father wouldn't consider the idea. "She never even knew Cora. Besides, Helen and her husband are hardly in need of money, with their smart house and their two cars, their winter cruises. And I don't doubt that Cora will marry well—"

He didn't seem too sure that I would, by the speculative look in my direction. And while Aunt Helen and Mother were still quarrelling—arguing or discussing, they called it—about which daughter was prettier, cleverer, etc., Cora followed in the family footsteps. The doctor's daughter became a nurse and went off to London. My father was in the civil service, so I too followed in the family footsteps of clerical work, so to speak, and became a secretary. During one of my many jobs I met Derek, and after he proposed, followed him to London. As Cora's flat was conveniently near the studio, I moved in with her, to the family's satisfaction. Aunt Helen, according to Mother, was absolutely chagrined that "little Mab, who

hasn't anything special about her really"
should have landed a television star. In the
circumstances, she felt that nothing less
than head of the hospital would do for her
Cora. "At least our Cora will be able to
keep an eye on Mab," said Aunt Helen,
which proved how little one knows one's
own. Cora had not the slightest intention
of keeping an eye on anyone but Derek.
She was the original sex-kitten, claws,
teeth and all—but beautiful, and I did
envy her that.

By the time I had reached London, Cora
had decided that nursing wasn't really her
cup of tea, or hypodermic. At least not
dreary hospital work, since some rich
patient had told her she was wasted there
with her looks and he was a theatrical
agent, so why didn't he sign her on to his
books. She was easily persuaded to do a
modelling-cum-theatrical job and did very
well for a time until she got bored with
walk-on parts that showed off her excellent
legs. She returned to part-time private
nursing, rich patients, and between
engagements haunted the agent for
auditions, longing like a hundred other
stage-struck girls for the big break and

instead landing an occasional role in a "cast of thousands" epic for screen or television.

"She has a rich patient at the moment," I told Derek. "And as a matter of fact, she has hopes of him—I mean matrimonial hopes."

Derek scowled. "Girl with her talent throwing herself away on an invalid."

"Don't worry, Cora never threw away anything that was useful—and I gather he might be good for a few years yet." I wished I didn't sound so catty, but whenever Derek talked about Cora—perhaps I was over-sensitive, but it seemed that he *smiled*. And worst of all, in a roomful of people, or with only me, as soon as Cora made her entrance, he went all broody and forgot who he was talking to or lost the place in the conversation in the effort to attract her attention. It happened once with Sam Wannamaker, and I could have died of shame.

When we reached the flat, Cora was sprawled on the sofa reading *Vogue*. Her hair needed washing, but even without make-up she managed to look breathtaking in a tatty old dressing-gown, that I would have prayed not to be found dead in.

"Your day off?" muttered Derek, smiling again.

"Today and forever—I'm resting."

"Resting? Have you lost your job again?" Oh dear, how accusing I sounded, just like a prim old aunt.

"Not quite. You might say the job has lost me." She paused to light a long dark cigarette, which was in keeping with her latest image.

"What happened?"

"Patient most inconsiderately died on me—poor old fella," she added hastily, "so I'm out in the cold again. We shall not starve, we who stand and wait, though. Cora is doing the decent thing and signing on the bureau."

Derek laughed as if this was the wittiest speech he'd heard in years. "Well, well— what a girl you are." When he had regained his equilibrium he said: "How would you like to go down to Wynsley Manor?"

"Oh-ho," she said. Even without the false eyelashes, her come-hither look was stunning. "This is so sudden. You did say

45

Wynsley? Tell me could this be the long-lost family seat?"

"William Frederick Brown's family didn't even have seats to their trousers—you *must* be joking. And their origins are lost without trace, thank God," said Derek, laughing. I noticed that he wasn't at all sensitive about Cora knowing that Wynsley was only his stage name. He looked at me. "As a matter of fact, this piece of property is your cousin's—or will be when she pays the first instalment."

Cora's eyebrows shot up—an arc of astonishment. "Mab! What have you been up to?"

"Derek is over-acting again," I said, throwing a little spanner into all this sweetness and light. "We have just rented an Elizabethan manor which *I* am going to occupy until the wedding—"

"Until which time I do the decent honourable thing—which, sweet cos-to-be, is where you come in," said Derek to Cora. "As you know, my marital arrangements are sticky to say the least, and until the divorce, modesty and Liz's private detective agency require that your cousin here, my bride-to-be, must be adequately chaperoned—"

"To cut a long story short," I interrupted somewhat impatiently, "seeing that you'll need to find a new flatmate when I leave, how would you like to give up the flat and come to Wynsley—"

She was enchanted with the idea, and half an hour later was already phoning her friends. "I may not commute for very long, of course. I expect there'll be rich patients in Abchester."

Derek and I exchanged glances. We didn't want to dampen her enthusiasm. After he left for the studio, bowing himself out in one of his Sir Amyas gestures which almost tumbled him down the narrow stairs and had an empty cereal packet, deftly aimed by Cora, to accompany his undignified flight, I made coffee and told her all about Wynsley Manor.

"Is it haunted?" I said no, and she looked gloomy. "What a pity. It won't be the same without a ghost. All the best Elizabethan houses have them. Goes with the panelling, the priest's hole, the terrible family secret—"

"You read too many romances. It isn't like that in real life, I assure you."

And of course, Cora—and Wynsley Manor—proved me wrong.

3

WE had hardly closed the door behind us and set down our cases when Cora was staring up the great staircase, sniffing the air like a deer-hind at bay.

"Know something?" she said triumphantly. "There is quite definitely a presence."

"A presence?" asked Derek, unused to Cora's supernatural terminology.

"From the other world—yes."

"Oh, you mean a ghost," said Derek cheerfully. "Expect the place is full of them."

"I get the definite impression of a man."

"Hmm. Competition, eh?" laughed Derek. "Well, another female would be more than I could cope with. I expect to have my hands full with two."

"What an unfortunate choice of words," said Cora, knowing she was being teased. However, with no wish to lose caste in

Derek's eyes, she added: "It's a benign presence, so we've nothing to fear."

"You mean that *you* have nothing to fear," said Derek fondly.

She gave him a dazzling smile, a small inclination of her head indicating that she was pleased and flattered. "Not to worry, Cora will protect you. She's not psychic for nothing. And ghosts never worried Mab—that old house of theirs on the Roman Wall was haunted as hell, but Mab never had a single manifestation. I was terrified out of my wits, I can tell you—gave me the creeps—it even *smelled* haunted—"

"How did it manage that? I've never heard of anyone smelling a ghost."

"Dead leaves—mould—the smell of old churches, musty Bibles—"

"Sounds like dry rot to me."

"It couldn't be haunted," I interrupted. "It wasn't even an old house—built about 1910."

"Did you ever see anything?" Derek asked Cora.

She shuddered. "No, nor did I want to. There was always mist—or a wind blowing—you could almost hear the Roman legions marching along—"

Derek smiled. "Well, my dear, I'm glad you're the one in the family with all the imagination. Not Mab here—or we'd be in trouble, especially as she'll be spending a lot of time alone." He looked around, shook his head. "Can't say I feel a thing. Do you, Mab?"

I didn't—only warmth and affection for the place that was to be my new home. However, when we were alone, Derek asked me how reliable Cora was. He'd obviously been more impressed than he pretended.

"Cora has certainly had some strange experiences—not only with one ghost, but with a whole legion of them. She saw Roman soldiers once at Housesteads and thought they were film extras. Turned out to be the Ninth Legion. Same thing happened on a holiday in Greece. Afterwards she realised she'd had a ringside seat at the Battle of Thermopylae."

I was inclined to take Cora's hauntings lightly. There had been so many throughout the years. Whenever we had taken family holidays in boarding houses or gloomy hotels, they were, according to Cora, so thick with ghosts that their owners would have had fits at entertaining so many invisible non-paying guests. In childhood, I thought she invented them to frighten me or just to give herself a feeling of superiority. When we grew older, I wasn't quite so sure.

"That's all right, then," said Derek. "I don't want you frightened by all her nonsense. Putting ideas into your head—however, you seem to know how to deal with them. I presume it'll be safe enough to leave her alone here when we're away."

"Oh, yes, she's banking on it. She's even brought along her Ouiji board, hoping to enliven the evenings with one-woman seances. Don't spoil her fun."

Derek shuddered. "Funny way for a lovely girl like her to get her kicks." He looked at his watch. "We'll have to be on our way by six in the morning. I'll have to trot off to bed soon. Happy, darling?" he said, and took me in his arms.

I had set my alarm and worked out exactly how long it would take us to get to Sir Amyas's next location—Haddon Hall in Derbyshire. I closed my eyes and could hardly sleep for the excitement of being in a four-poster bed—even in solitary splendour. I expected to have thrilling and exciting dreams, especially after Cora's predictions.

That first night in Wynsley was a bitter disappointment. It held no warning dreams, and all I awoke to was the discovery that somewhere during the hours of darkness I had developed a shocking head cold. As soon as I raised my head I began to sneeze, and by the time I had staggered down to the kitchen, my nose was in competition with the taps in the sink. Streaming and blowing, I leaned against the pantry door, my head throbbing.

"What on earth is wrong with you?" asked Derek, watching my attempts to set the table.

"I've got a code, I tink—"

"You certainly have. When did this happen?" Without waiting for a reply, he seized the loaf of bread. "For God's sake, let me make the toast—you'll cover everything with germs—I don't want to be contaminated—honestly, just looking at you, I can feel them crawling all over me in their millions."

I sat opposite him, as far away as possible, and tried to control and disguise my condition, which was worsening by the moment. After hearing me sneezing and blowing as accompaniment to two cups of strong coffee, Derek threw down his toast and marmalade in disgust.

"I think I'll have to go alone, Mab. It's out of the question. I mean, I can't afford the luxury of catching your cold at a time like this."

"You bay have it already," I said with evil relish. "After all, I brobably had it last night—"

Poor Derek almost leaped into the air. He lived in constant terror of taking cold when he was filming and in general was good to himself, conscientiously nursing headaches and stomach pains and every sign of increasing age which taunts actors approaching forty. His faith in new drugs and patent medicines was both touching and childlike—the only naive thing about him.

"If only it had been some other day." Derek was superstitious about driving himself to rehearsals on the 13th. Three times on the eve of a new series, he had been involved in minor accidents which delayed him—and production—and created all hell and chaos in the studio. I suspected that it wasn't fate but more likely lack of attention and brooding on his lines. Anyway, one of my secretarial duties was to drive him on location and leave him time to concentrate on Sir Amyas, as he called it. I could see his problem—the Porsche Carrera with its intimate atmosphere was no place for a sneezing germ-ridden companion.

"I suppose I could take Cora along instead. She's a good driver."

Before I could put a name to the half-dozen or so reasons why I didn't think it was a good idea for Cora to go in my place, none of which would have convinced Derek in the slightest, seeing they were based on that female instinct for survival —intuition—Cora had appeared in the kitchen with almost suspicious alacrity and was demanding: "Who is taking my name in vain?"

"Mab has developed a terrible cold. How would you like to drive me up to

Derbyshire instead?" asked Derek. He was smiling again.

Cora was delighted to oblige. They were both very kind and fussed over me. Now that he had found such an admirable substitute as chauffeuse, Derek was restored to his normal good humour and offered to drop by the vicarage to see Mrs. Timmons.

"She's a nice old bird and she'll come up and look after you—if I ask her."

Mrs. Timmons was barmaid-cum-housekeeper at the Wynsley Arms, and Derek had acquired her last night when he went down for a bottle of wine and cigarettes. She was a great fan of Sir Amyas and charmed that he was to be living, as she called it, "just across the field." She was home help at the Manse and would be pleased to further extend her activities on Tuesday and Thursday to help out at Wynsley.

I was too reduced by my sneezing and blowing to protest. I couldn't even summon up enough energy to be wildly jealous as I watched them drive away. Scornfully refusing their advice that bed was the best possible place, I assured them it was just a cold and I preferred to be Spartan. It would take its course whether I nursed it or ignored it—and I preferred to do the latter.

"It's your funeral," said Cora, who was feeling put out that I had refused all her little boxes of pills and remedies.

When they disappeared from sight, I decided that the first stage in fighting the cold was to pretend it didn't exist and busy myself with unpacking some of the boxes containing household effects which had arrived with the furniture, sent on by Mr. Willis. To this end I devoted my morning, and when I stopped at ten-thirty to make coffee, I discovered that I hadn't sneezed or blown my nose once since they departed. The horrendous head cold had disappeared as suddenly as it had appeared.

"Mirabel—Mirabel." Someone called my name.

"Yes," I answered automatically—and then I looked up the staircase. That was the direction it had come from, but there was no one. I would have been terrified had there been someone when I thought about it afterwards. At that moment there was a ring at the front door and I opened it with considerable relief to a plump middle-aged lady with her hair in rollers and shrouded by a chiffon scarf.

"I'm Mrs. Timmons, dear. Mr. Wynsley asked me to look in and see you —he said you were poorly. He was that worried, the poor man. Well," she put hands on hips and studied me carefully. "I'm pleased to see you're better than I expected to see you. Men are all the same, aren't they, dear? My Joe's like your Mr. Wynsley, sees everything in the small print. Such bears with sore heads if they have an ache or pain, think us women are just the same. If they only knew *all* that women have to put up with," she added, rolling her eyes heavenward. "From cradle to grave, it's just one thing after another—"

"Yes, of course," I interrupted hastily. "I really am fine. However, I'm pleased Mr. Wynsley asked you to call—er, do you want to start this morning?"

"Oh, Lord love you, no, dear. I'm with the Vicar this morning—just popped round to introduce myself and if you were abed, make you a nice cuppa. However," she poked her head around, staring past me into the hall, "I can see you're all nicely organised. See you tomorrow at nine. I expect there'll be a lot to see to before the wedding—Mr. Wynsley said you would be getting married very soon." She smiled, head to one side, sizing me up. "My goodness, but a lot of girls *and* older ladies too must envy you. Such a lovely man, your fiancé—and a lot handsomer off the screen even than he is on it. Well, Miss Fenwick," she held out her hand, beaming: "I'm sure we're going to get along fine. I like to feel that I'm a friend to my ladies—and I do a little plain cooking in the evenings sometimes, if you're entertaining—"

"Thank you, that's most kind—"

"Fenwick's an unusual name in these parts. North country, isn't it? I had an Uncle Ben Fenwick from over Durham way."

I declined relationship. However, as she was leaving, I said: "Did you have difficulty in getting the doorbell to work? We had awful trouble the first time."

"Oh, no, you came right away."

"You didn't call my name then?" I felt embarrassed at the question.

"Miss Fenwick, you mean?"

"No—my first name."

She smiled. "Now, I wouldn't do that, miss—I know my place—besides, I don't know what your first name is, do I?"

"It's Mirabel—but most people call me Mab."

"Mirabel—how strange."

"Strange?"

She shrugged quickly. "Yes. An unusual name isn't it?" But her eyes evaded mine, and I was sure that some other reason had surprised her. Suddenly she dived a hand into her capacious shopping bag. "Almost forgot, dear. Mrs. Brownlee—Vicar's wife—said you might like a read of this. But could she have it back straight away as there isn't another copy. See you tomorrow, then."

"Make it Thursday, please. I have to go to Abchester tomorrow."

She frowned. "Now don't go overtaxing yourself. Look after that cold."

I thanked her and went inside with the slim volume, printed about eighty years before, neither particularly rare nor interesting to anyone but the member of an old family who is ready to pay to see his family history in print. In a long-winded and unnecessary introduction the author, Geoffrey Wynsley, a member of a firm of solicitors in Abchester, went into considerable details of the architecture of the house including a reproduction of a painting now in the local museum at Abchester, reputed to be Wynsley Manor before the fire had destroyed the central block and the west wing. I learned that the museum also contained, on permanent loan, many of the more valuable family portraits and historic possessions. That, I decided, would be worth a visit.

I am still at a loss to recall in any detail how I filled in those hours of my first day alone at Wynsley. There are some weird gaps, and in the light of later events, it was as if from the beginning, time played tricks on me. Later, common sense—and Derek—argued that despite my illusion that the head cold had vanished, I was possibly feverish with a temperature for a couple of days, to which Cora added a nurse's opinion that possibly I sat down and dozed off in a chair without really noticing. She decided that the mysterious cold was an allergy, a bout of hay fever. Apparently I was allergic to something in the master bedroom which I occupied. Or was it to the dust, since there was considerably more than I normally dealt with in a London flat—or even on the Roman Wall, come to think of it. Dust came out of long-closed cupboards in clouds and descended from the back of shelves with a vast, scampering army of spiders which had been safe from the hands of man or woman and free to make their webs for hundreds of insect generations.

Sometimes in my activities I stopped, aware of a strange sensation in my head, a buzzing—or were there noises just far enough off-stage to engage my attention. At various periods throughout the day I thought I heard a bell ring—the old-fashioned clanging ones used to summon servants from the kitchen basement. Once there were many whispering voices, as though children were rushing downstairs, laughing and whispering to each other. The hall was empty. I opened the door expecting to see them outside, running across the orchard to the meadow.

It was very disturbing but I wasn't frightened—not yet. However, even sure that there must be some logical explanation, I decided that this lonely old house was no place for me suddenly to develop an excessive imagination, and as the shadows of my first day lengthened, I was determined to be sensible. The only sure way to rid oneself of irritating noises was to create greater ones, so I switched on the transistor radio and listened to the reassuring though suddenly raucous sounds of that world I had abandoned— only yesterday? That in itself was astonishing, for it felt as if London already belonged to another world, to another page of history, as yet unborn.

The large kitchen with its central heating unit in one corner was an anachronism, but comforting on a chilly summer evening, and I decided that here I would stay until Derek and Cora returned. It seemed absurd to take a book away into the drawing room. Eventually I found a concert of Haydn on a foreign station, since pop music had never sounded more out of place than in this gentle setting with the evening sun dappling the orchard, the bird-song deep and luscious and the trees gathering themselves into the immobility of sleep, so that no breeze disturbed their tranquillity. Even as I watched, a pale thin mist moved up from the wooded valley and wrapped the horizons in a sheltering cloak. So many summers, I thought, since this house began, so many evenings exactly like this one.

Night is my best time of the day, and my parents always complain that I rarely go to bed on the same day as I rise from it. But suddenly, although nine had struck, I was tired, already yawning. Blaming the allergy and the change of air, I went upstairs to my bedroom, taking with me a thermos of coffee, since I could not imagine sleeping more than six hours. I also took my Wynsley book, since I normally could not sleep without reading for a while. I dared the lower half of the dinosaur for a quick bath, and feeling deliciously regal, retired to my monumental bed. It had been here for four hundred years, I thought, inspecting its carved posts and canopy—from the very beginning of this house it had seen innumerable births, deaths and begettings. There was something very comfortiong about its solidity, about lying there propped up against the pillows to read about all the Wynsleys who had occupied this very bed through the ages.

"The original site of the present Wynsley Manor was occupied by the ancient Priory of Our Saviour. At the Reformation, Henry the Eighth gave its lands and charter and most of its wealth to one of his esquires, Sir Robert Wynsley, who had a modest house and estate next to the Priory. Sir Robert expressed his gratitude by frequently entertaining his King and Court, including on more than one occasion the future Queen, Anne Boleyn, who gave to Sir Robert an embroidered glove bearing her initials which can be seen to this day in the Museum at Abchester. No trace of the Priory which his son Sir Francis Wynsley demolished remains, nor has the secret passage been found which was said to link the Priory and the original Wynsley Manor to the Saxon Church of Our Saviour. Presumably Sir Robert's original modest house was incorporated into the present dwellings. All that remains of his pre-Reformation estate is the old tower on the hill of Wynsley, which can be dated to the time of Richard the First, who gave to Gilles de Wynsley lands for accompanying him faithfully to the Crusades. Gilles also returned from Jerusalem bearing a reliquary said to contain a piece of the Sacred Cross and ordered that the Church of Our Saviour be added to the crude Saxon church to house this sacred treasure said to have miraculous healing powers.

"When King Henry's wife, Jane Seymour, lay dying after the birth of her son Edward, Sir Robert 'borrowed' the reliquary and presented it to his King—alas, too late to divert the course of history. When the parish priest protested at this piece of sacrilege, Sir Robert, who was known to have an uncertain temper, struck him with such savagery that he fell and burst open his head upon the altar stone.

"Dying, he said: 'As my brains spill forth, so shall all of thine. As violently I died, so shall all of thine—'

"It seemed that the ancient Wynsleys

were cursed with incipient madness, although many of their endings smack of coincidence and the readiness of the superstitious to relate such incidents to a supernatural cause.

"Sir Francis the Builder was a wellknown practical joker, and according to records of the time, Wynsley Manor—in particular the central block and west wing, alas, destroyed by fire in the eighteenth century—was honeycombed with secret panels and passages, as Sir Francis loved to leap out, to appear and disappear before his terrified and surprised guests. He was particularly fond of access panels in bedrooms, a voyeur who also had an unfortunate partiality to watching the toilets of ladies staying in the house and the more intimate relationships upon which the veil of discretion ought to remain suspended, offending by his subsequent repetition of what had taken place under his roof, the very decencies of human nature.

"Sir Charles, his eighteenth century descendant, put these access panels to even more sinister purpose, being a member of the Hellfire Club and an experimenter with demonology—"

An experimenter with demonology. My eyelids were weighed down with lead, the words on the page blurred before me. I slept.

I awoke next morning considerably refreshed. My dreams had been mercifully untroubled by the wicked Wynsleys or by sleeping in the very bed that many of them had doubtless occupied in all their strange and sinister moods.

I opened the bedroom window. It was six o'clock, but the birds and the sun had already been abroad for some time. I looked over to my right, to the tower on the hill where Henry the Eighth had dallied with poor Anne Boleyn away from the watchful eyes of his rightful wife, Catherine of Aragon. I thought suddenly of Derek's Liz and her private detective agency, although they had once loved each as now did Derek and I. How little human nature has changed through the centuries and how easily desire turns to boredom, and boredom to hate.

In the kitchen everything was as I had left it the night before, although as I looked around I felt that the dust of time was already beginning to gather on the shelves, the bread had turned stale, and there would be the mould of months creeping across the marmalade newly-opened the previous morning. Yesterday morning Derek and Cora had gone to Derbyshire and I had a cold in the head. But was it really yesterday, or had I entered a Rip van Winkle world where time itself had gone awry, and the clock was running backwards through the centuries and taking me with it—

The idea was so unnerving, even the blaring inconsistencies of the transistor radio failed to reassure me. The voices sounded stale, the jokes were weary, and the records told of weary love and the broken vows of a dying race. I gulped down my coffee and escaped into the sunlight.

4

THE climb up to the old tower through the bright meadows of a summer morning restored my courage. I was no longer alone in the dead world of yesterday, some grim survivor of a trick of time. I was myself, greeted cheerily by lads cutting early hay. A rabbit scampered almost across my feet, and an army of starlings ceased their chirping on a telegraph wire long enough to watch my progress respectfully.

At last, breathless from the unusual effort of picking a way through paths no longer visible to humans and only recorded in the instincts of smaller animals, I reached my vantage point. The walls of the tower were already warm under my hand, and that was comforting, for this was still an alien land. However, it was growing less so, and one day it would claim me as its own. As I looked down the hill history seemed to fade into insignificance as I remembered that this land must have looked the same through Boadicea's eyes as it did through mine, give or take away a few forests. The gentle undulating hills, the tiny domesticated valleys rich with farmland and cattle seemed to exist within living memory of watermills, the rolling black heath sinister and dark, haunted by almost forgotten legends. I wondered what legends the ruined tower held.

Above every belt of trees grew a tall stone spire to tell man that this life and all its beauty was but a step on the way to immortality. There were other spires like that at Wynsley—All that remained of the once flourishing hamlet dominated by the manor house and feudal barons of old time. I could see as far as Abchester, its ugly red brick straining at the leash but mercifully softened by distance into a rose-red mass perched by a riverbank laden with trees. Away to the left, cars ran in straight lines, important and going some-where, like a myriad army of varicoloured ants, the busy motorway only a smear of sunlight in the glow of morning, the noise of traffic as distant and inoffensive as the buzz of summer insects, yawning and stretching their wings in every bush around me.

I loved this morning of the world, sweet and pure, with not a hint of pollution in its wine-sharp air. I didn't want to know the blue haze on the far horizon and the great sprawl of a city. Let it remain anonymous. Towns had no place in this world of lanes, secret and secure. I walked back through the long grasses, picking my way before me along forgotten paths, turning corners that had once led into soft sleepy villages, with sunlit glades and far-off dense hornbeam trees. And suddenly I knew I was lost, lost in a bewildering maze of vanished paths, all their one-time directions securely barred by brisk and efficient barbed-wire fences.

I climbed one, to the considerable detriment of my trousers, and found that the labyrinth continued in like manner and that I was in a valley which gave no hint of man's domain. The barriers seemed to guard against trespassers who, like myself, must have been only the rare idiots who lost their way.

And then I saw him—a horseman riding hard against the sun. He was only two hundred yards away from me but it might well have been two hundred miles across that impenetrable landscape. I could see the sun glint on pale hair—blond or grey—a white shirt haloed with light, its sleeves billowing, and a dark horse's mane.

My heart leaped with recognition. Of course, this was the man I had seen riding past the orchard, the same rider whom neither Derek nor Mr. Willis had glimpsed, due to their poor eyesight. I remembered the first time that evening—was it just a week ago—when he had leaned out of the window at Wynsley Manor, for some instinct told me this was the same man.

"Hello—hello?" I called. Surely he would be able to direct me out of the tangle. "Hello there—hello—help!" But the gliding graceful movement of horse and rider never faltered. I waved my arms hopefully, but he hadn't seen me. It was too bad, but before feeling indignation I had to remember that to a horseman the sounds of harness and hoofs probably drown out shouts from a couple of fields away.

At least I wasn't alone in the world. And

where the horseman was there was probably a road, and that road leading back to Wynsley. I took courage, and fighting my way through the long grasses, stumbled on in the direction he had taken. Occasionally my progress was further impeded by giant slabs of mossy stones tangled in briars and weeds.

An angel's face, its features almost vanished under a fuzzy growth of lichen, stared up from my feet, and with the first scalp-tingle of horror I had thus far experienced, I realised I was walking through a disused cemetery, and a very old one at that. Even the sunlight, the birdsong, the great trees, brought no comfort. I was in the presence of long-ago death and dusty and crumbling skeletons. Panic seized me —I stopped and listened. A sound, what was it?—the old man with the scythe. Through a thinner part of the thicket, a clearing and a black shape in a long gown moved. I thrust my way through and found myself on the edge of more tomb-stones, upright and some of them new, and the black-gowned figure turned, saw me and waved.

"This way—this way. Lost, were you?"

I emerged, feeling like Red Riding Hood after a narrow escape from the wolf, from the sinister world of my imagination into the normality of scented grass-cuttings as the Vicar of the Church of Our Saviour wielded a twentieth-century electric lawn mower.

"Be with you in a moment," he shouted, and relieved to be released from my hobgoblin world, I watched him happily in this most ordinary of summertime British occupation, trimming the lawns. I found his occupational territory included not only the Vicarage ones, manicured and daintily bordered with neat plants, but also respectfully close to the tombstones, where the mounds of grass were uneven and the motor growled away furiously, screeching at the larger tufts of grass. Occasionally the Vicar turned and darted me a look of helpless embarrassment which humorously denoted he had doubts about what the occupant under the tombstone must be thinking about all this activity. At other times he stopped, stared earnestly as if reading the inscription, his lips moving as though some apology were necessary to the stone-winged guardian of the departed.

Then, smiling, he would take out a large hankie, mop his brow, adjust his specs, and move on.

I could have watched him all day, sniffing the heady smell of new-mown grass in this lovely setting, tranquil and refreshing, with the promise of a hot summer afternoon. I was about to move on towards the Vicarage and head in the direction of home, when he stopped and beckoned me over.

"Finished now."

I made my way toward him down a path narrower even than that associated with virtue. He beamed upon my progress and held out his hand.

"Of course you must be Miss Fenwick, from Wynsley." He made it sound very important. "You've recovered from your nasty cold, I see. My wife was coming along to see you this afternoon, bearing a little soup and nourishment. She will be so pleased to see you up and about again. Sorry to have kept you waiting, but I only have the loan of the mower from down the road and there is so much to do. But I try to keep abreast of it all." He looked somewhat reproachfully toward the tombstones as though they offended by the mortal sin of untidiness. "And of course, when the Manor was unoccupied and I had my machine here, we have always trundled across. It seemed a shame to let the wilderness creep up to the very windows—"

There was the sound of a bell somewhere at hand. "Ah, that'll be Margaret— a cup of coffee's ready. I trust you will join us, my dear—There's a short cut." He led the way briskly through another maze of grasses on to a tiny path, stopping to direct me. "No, not that way—this— allow me, please. Follow on—"

"I'm afraid I got lost in the old churchyard."

"So I observed, my dear. A nasty experience. It's very old, hasn't been used in two hundred years, but you could have given your ankle a nasty turn—some of the sunken graves can cause accidents for the unwary."

"Is that why they put up the barbed wire?"

"Yes, after two children fell in and, alas, were not discovered for some time. They should not have been there in the first place, of course, but their parents were very cross. Holiday-makers they were, with a caravan." He sighed. "The grass really gets beyond me in the summer." He nodded towards tombstones which stared out of the nearer wilderness. "You will have doubtless observed in your short perambulations that there are more of the dear departed than the living in our little community. Do feel free to explore. Some of the tombstones are very old—and there is a Wynsley vault. I'm sure the family would be delighted, pleased that you were interested."

I didn't ask whether he was referring to the present or past members of the Wynsley family. I had a strange feeling that for him and his faith—which I envied —death was but a temporary parting, an inconvenience, on a longer journey. I was glad I had met him, a darling old man, so much a part of his setting too, in the dusty cassock with his tonsured head. Tonsured by nature and not by design, a fringe of white hair grew thickly between ears and neck. His rosy smiling face suggested someone—a Friar Tuck out of his time, I thought triumphantly. One almost expected the crucifix dangling from the robe.

The vicarage was mid-Victorian, its sacred functions adhered to by the builder's passion for arched windows and doorways and for stained glass windows inappropriately placed. I felt that the Vicar and his wife must have rarely forgotten their churchly function as they took tea in rooms which more resembled ancient vestries than normal domestic apartments. I followed him through a dark, narrow hall up a creaking staircase into a book-lined study which was straight out of Edgar Allan Poe. Ghostly marbled heads, their whiteness softened by a film of dust, stared down at us from the semi-darkness of the tops of tall bookcases. Old books and manuscripts tumbled from every corner, and where there was no more room on shelves, were stacked upon the floor. And dominating this scene of Gothic splendour, complete with ravens and falcons, cruel-beaked under glass, entombed with their victims for all time, was a modern type-writer, brisk and shining and electric.

Mr. Brownlee stared at the birds. "They are not mine, but my predecessor was an antiquarian and naturalist. I'd like to give them to the Museum at Abchester, but it seems they have more than enough stuffed birds and animals. They make me feel rather uncomfortable. Don't you think there is something reproachful in their attitudes?"

Before I could answer, the creaking stairs and a shuddering sound of china indicated another arrival. The door opened on Mrs. Brownlee bearing a pot of freshly made coffee and a plate of newly baked scones, their tall sides bursting with raspberry jam and cream. I was suddenly aware of hunger, of my perfunctory breakfast.

Mrs. Brownlee asked sympathetically after my cold, seemed surprised that all my symptoms had disappeared so quickly, and agreed with my allergy theory. I thanked her for the book and promised to return it as soon as I had finished it. She agreed with me that it was very interesting and asked how much I had read.

As we talked I accepted more coffee and more than one scone. "I'm so pleased to see you have an appetite, Miss Fenwick. That you are not one of those young ladies who spend their time refusing all goodies on the grounds of dieting. It is one of the fashions of our time to be constantly counting calories."

"One can understand that, my dear," said her husband, "when every year the trousers become tighter and the blouses more revealing."

We all laughed, and I thought how lucky were his parishioners to have such a human priest, conscious of but never condemning the vanities of others. They were a delightful couple with the strange family resemblance that comes, I have often observed, through years of living together. A plump, comfortable couple, Mrs. Brownlee gained on hair and her abundant waves were crisply silver, but their faces were robin-like, bright of eye and cheek. I was not surprised to hear that they loved the open outdoor life, and spent as much time as Mr. Brownlee could spare away from this book-lined study. To Mrs. Brownlee's sensible tweed skirt, I could see ankle socks and sturdy boots on occasion as she clambered across the heath at her husband's side, armed with walking-sticks and rucksacks, his clerical collar abandoned for a sporty sweater on windy autumn days, sometimes talking, sometimes in the companionable silence that belongs to those who have spent more than half a lifetime together.

There were pictures of a boy and girl in graduation robes, wedding groups and babies in prams or stiffly miserable in studio portraits. They were, I discovered, grandparents several times over. I looked at this devoted, happy couple and envied them. Would Derek and I be like this some day, perhaps even rousing that "look-alike" sensation in the strangers we met? I felt a dark shadow move across the sun, cutting off the warmth from my shoulders as I sat by the window. It was like a warning, a chill premonition that my love for Derek could never be. My fairy-tale romance with Sir Amyas Symon was as unreal as one of his television episodes —and likely to be as brief. I thought of him with Cora, smiling, forgetting me— trying to find the words to say it was all over, a mistake—I saw myself sitting in a lonely room, empty, heartbroken—

And there was Mrs. Brownlee smiling

too, putting into words the story I saw as already ended:

"My husband tells me you are to marry Derek Wynsley—the famous Derek Wynsley. How romantic—"

"My wife is an addict—she almost wrote to the telly people—had to be restrained, in fact—when she discovered that she was going to miss an episode as the new times coincided with choir practice."

Mrs. Brownlee laughed. "You do exaggerate, dear. Actually, Miss Fenwick, I did nag the choir-master a little, until he set practice back an hour later. It was very naughty of me," she giggled, "but Sir Amyas is such fun."

"My wife is very romantic," said Mr. Brownlee with an affectionate glance.

"Then you must come up to Wynsley and have a meal with us when Derek— and my cousin, who is living with us meantime—return."

"Oh, we would love that. We often wondered if he was connected with the family, and it did seem a coincidence that he should come and live here. We're most impressed to have such a distinguished neighbour."

I explained that it was alas, only his stage name, that he had to find something unusual and happened to be driving through Wynsley.

"And he chose our little village—how romantic. It has certainly put us on the map." She looked at me with the smiling curiosity I noticed in other women. It asked, clearer than any words, what mysterious qualities of sex appeal and femininity I possessed under my somewhat ordinary exterior, to lure such an exciting lover. Yes, I thought, even the Vicar's wife—she's human enough to wonder.

I discovered that the Brownlees had come here ten years ago after leaving the busy London parish where the Vicar had, not surprisingly, taken a coronary. "He never had a moment's rest, night and day—"

"That is what being a servant of God is all about, my dear," her husband said, a little reprovingly. "I was just getting too old for the job, that's all. And I certainly am allowed to take it easy here. A little gentle exercise, my forays in summertime with the electric mower. And my wife's care and attention," again the sidelong affectionate glance. "All any man really needs."

"You could do with paying more attention to your waistline," said Mrs. Brownlee. "He used to be thin as a reed," she added, with a little laugh. "Anyway, Miss Fenwick, I hope you and your future husband will settle in Wynsley and be as happy as we have been."

I explained that we had only rented the manor. "We are hoping to buy, but we cannot make an offer until the present owner is traced." I found myself taking refuge in the royal "we." Derek would never forgive me if he felt I had even hinted to people that Wynsley Manor was to belong to me.

"Have we ever met him, dear?" asked Mrs. Brownlee.

"No, I don't think he's ever set eyes on the place."

"He didn't ever visit Miss Wynsley. I thought—"

"No, never," said Mr. Brownlee. "He only inherited when the old lady died. He is one of the world's wanderers. I gather he has no settled home although he is an American citizen. He's an explorer, and as such, I can't see him wanting to settle here. I don't think you should encounter any difficulties there. These American gentlemen of action are always very highly-powered."

"And being a Wynsley, I expect he has the family characteristics of being a little odd, too," volunteered Mrs. Brownlee.

Her husband darted her a disapproving glance, as though she had said too much to a stranger.

"Did you know Miss Wynsley well?" I asked them.

"Hardly at all." And the faintest of shadows passed over the two cheerful faces, as Mr. Brownlee added: "We were here at the time, of course—"

"The time?"

"Yes, when she was alive, but I couldn't honestly say we ever had more than a passing acquaintance with her. She wasn't a churchgoer, and although my wife tried to interest her in some of the social activities one would expect the lady of the manor to enjoy, she received a rather unenthusiastic response—"

"The usual response I received, Miss Fenwick, was the front door opened a couple of inches and promptly slammed in my face. Or if she happened to be upstairs, she'd lean out of the window and demand what I wanted as if she didn't know who I was, and I was selling old clothes or something."

"It was very distressing for my wife," said the Vicar. "And quite uncalled for. Even in a recluse, if she is a woman of breeding, one expects good manners."

"I used to worry about her, living there all alone in that vast house. Then one day, poor soul, she must have taken a giddy turn and leaned out of the window upstairs and over-balanced—" She shook her head significantly.

"Most distressing," said the Vicar. "You might offer Miss Fenwick another scone. Come along, my dear—do have the last one. Although a thousand a year as the old adage says isn't much in anyone's language these days, at least you can be sure of the handsome husband. While you're here, you might like our leaflet about our old church—that is, if you are —er—of our persuasion—"

As Mr. Brownlee bounded to his feet and foraged among nests of papers, Mrs. Brownlee sat silent and I had the oddest feeling that the atmosphere had changed. The conversation had been steered too abruptly, they were too eager to leave Miss Wynsley and get back on to the safe ground of scones and coffee and the church.

I felt the Vicar was too eager about the leaflet. It was not to be found. There would be some in the vestry, and he would bring it over to the Manor later. He beamed upon us. "And now, my dears, I fear I must get to work again."

It was my cue for departure. At the front door I thanked them both and said: "Would you please satisfy my rather morbid curiosity?" Before they could demur, I said, "What happened to Miss Wynsley?"

A guarded look was exchanged, and I was sorry that I had caused that mere flicker of annoyance, as slight as the action of brushing off a spirited wasp who keeps returning to the attack. "I thought you knew," said the Vicar. "The unfortunate lady broke her neck when she fell out of the window."

"She wasn't the first one at Wynsley to do that either—it is almost a family tradition."

"Don't exaggerate, my dear—of course it isn't. One or two have done so—but the windows *are* high and the flagstones are hard. When you have children—in a few years—I would advise bars on some of those windows, to prevent accidents."

They still hadn't answered my question. "What I really meant is, was she buried here at Wynsley?"

"Yes. In the family vault—over there." He indicated the graveyard. "The church contains a very handsome tomb of the Elizabethan Wynsleys, too, if you're interested."

Mrs. Brownlee followed me to the front gate. "If you aren't too busy settling in, come to the Flower Festival tomorrow. Sometime—perhaps next year—we will ask the famous Derek Wynsley to judge the floats."

From Geoffrey Wynsley's family history, I gathered that the Flower Festival was one of those originally pagan midsummer festivals which had been Christianised by the early Church and which after the Reformation had condemned such idolatry, had emerged in yet another guise. Yet still it seemed the people were loath to let go of the old ways, the old fertility rites. Now it consisted of people in hamlets for miles around who gathered with their decorated floats and fancy-dress costumes, representing a pageant of the ages. Traditionally it had been held at the manor house of Wynsley after being blessed at the Church. Now it began at Abchester, walked or rode the two miles to the Wynsley Arms where refreshments were provided. I got more than a hint that these refreshments were of the spirit kind, and out of a bottle.

I returned home clutching a bus time-table and a pot of newly made raspberry jam, whose excellence in the scones I had praised to the hilt. I must confess I drew a deep breath before opening the kitchen door, but everything was as it had been in my hasty flight, except that the sun had come round and made the whole room look cheerier, although I also realised it sadly needed decorating. At least now it existed in the right time. What an absurd idea that had been, I thought, putting on the coffee pot—a dignified name for lunch, which was all I could manage after that surfeit of Vicarage baking. I had just put down my empty cup and picked up Geoffrey Wynsley again when the phone, installed on the kitchen wall, began to peal with angry insistence.

"Hello, Mab?" It was Derek. "Where in heaven's name have you been? Why weren't you answering the phone? I've been nearly out of my mind—thought you must be lying there unconscious—I tried twice last night—"

"I went to bed at nine. I suppose I couldn't hear the phone upstairs."

"Nine—*you?* Good heavens, you must have been feeling dreadful. How's the cold?" I told him it was much better. "Where have you been this morning? I tried to get you before eight o'clock."

"I went out—just wandering about. I explored the old tower on the hill."

"Hmm—you aren't usually an early bird." A pause. "Is everything all right, Mab? Who have you got there?" he said suspiciously.

"I haven't got anyone here—it's the radio you're hearing. And I'm fine. How's the filming?" It was fine. "And Cora?" She was fine, too. The pips buzzed us, threatening to carry him off.

"I'll have to go—haven't any more tens. And I just nipped out—I'll ring later. Love you, darling—take care—"

I sat down feeling gratified and even, I might add, a little pleased that Derek had been worried enough to call several times. It was quite out of character. Normally, when he was being Sir Amyas, he hadn't time to give anyone else a single thought. I found myself smiling as I turned up the radio. A man was reading poetry—and Derek had been jealous. Fancy that.

I decided to make out a shopping list for Abchester and went over to the refrigerator.

"Mirabel." I heard my name clearly, turned and went back to the radio. I increased its volume. How strange. The reader must have mentioned my name, and I had selected it specially from his reading. There was no further reference, the reading ended, and a music programme took over.

I went into the study and arranged all my books. All my books which had seemed to overwhelm the flat and overflow from every corner, faded into insignificance on the imposing bookshelves.

I went into the drawing room ruefully contemplating chintz covers on big floppy sofas—comfortable, but not at all the decor the room with its handsome panelling and carved ceiling demanded. Derek was pleased with the effect, it gave him no qualms. He liked comfort. "You have no idea," he had told me, "how grotesquely uncomfortable real Tudor furniture can be. An hour of authentic Sir Amyas is enough for me—I have no desire to carry those chairs and tables on into real life. Small wonder they did all their entertaining from those vast four-posters, holding court and afternoon equivalents of our coffee parties. Bed was the only comfortable place in the house."

I regarded the setting through narrowed eyes, trying to feel at home in it, imagining it with a party going. Yes, a log fire, and roses in those huge copper bowls, would add a homey, welcoming touch. Later, there would be chrysanthemums, bringing with them the smell of autumn—and Christmas would be lovely, the best of all seasons in this room.

I decided that I would leave the study strictly alone. As Derek's province, he could add his own touches. Upstairs we would use only the master bedroom once we were married, and keep the others for guests. How unreal this future sounded as if putting it into words was just to reassure myself that the past and present which had filled these rooms, which had paled and darkened and fled taking with them joy and sorrow, were somehow related to that future which lay just around the corner.

The closed doors of the Long Gallery were a challenge. I was rather afraid, and determined not to be so. I opened them. Poor sad room. There was nothing sinister about it today. It was too ugly to be threatening. I walked over to the hideous long window which opened on to a minute wrought-iron balcony. I wondered what it had been used for, presuming plants. No one would ever have cared to step over the sill and sit there. I could understand the Vicar's concern about the safety of these windows. This one, at least, looked very dangerous. I looked around me—the least attractive room in the house—better for to have stripped it than to leave this travesty, the ravages of what was once so beautiful, the shattered corpse of all that remained after the fire. I tried to think of it before— stretching the length of the house, many-windowed and embrasured, carved and panelled, a showpiece grand enough for visiting royalty. In times of peril, a refuge, or in bad weather a place of exercise for the women of the house to walk back and forth, chattering, running dogs and children, laughing, shouting—the ring of footsteps.

Poor sad room, it was like some noted beauty, grown old and ugly and afraid of close scrutiny. It was cold and unhappy, quite the nastiest room in the house, yet it fascinated me. There was a challenge here. Perhaps some day that challenge would be declared and I would know the name of the adversary.

Closing the door upon its torments, I returned to the library, whose window seat upon the raised dais was charming in the sunshine. I decided to continue Geoffrey Wynsley's history so that I could return it to the Vicarage. Reading between the lines they were an unsavory lot, and I wondered how much of that mysterious fire which destroyed the main part of the house during one of the meetings of the Hellfire Club had been accidental. It sounded suspiciously as if some person or persons might have had good reason to wish to see the end of their arrogant feudal lord.

With the awareness of being observed, I looked out of the window, and there, leaning on the orchard gate, was the fair-haired horseman. For a few moments we stared across the garden, each wondering if the other had noticed. Then he raised a hand, saluted me gravely. I was pleased, and waved back. As he made no other move, curiosity got the better of me, and I decided to wander out as casually as possible and get a closer look at him. As I hastened through the kitchen, I saw from the window that he was still there, looking up at the house, the sleeves of his white shirt moving in the breeze, his hair ruffled across his brow. Even at fifty yards I was aware of an extremely attractive young man.

I opened the back door, and the movement caught his eye. He waved again, smiling, and I thought he called a greeting.

"Yes, gorgeous evening, isn't it?" I called.

He mouthed something like: "May I come in?" His hand was on the gate.

"Please do." I was delighted out of all proportion that I was going to meet my handsome stranger, for this was undoubtedly the man I had seen leaning out of the upstairs window. Even before I spoke to him, I had recognised that he had some intimate connection with the house, a feeling in my bones.

He had opened the gate and I was walking towards him, when inside the kitchen the phone rang. I stopped, knowing it was Derek. I felt suddenly angry and made a helpless gesture towards the door.

"Won't be a moment," I called. He watched me, smiling.

5

"YOU took your time," said Derek's voice accusingly as I picked up the phone.

"I was in the garden."

"How are you? How's the cold?"

I told him I was fine. He was fine and so was Cora. Filming was fine. I was bored, wanting to get back to my waiting visitor. I heard my answers getting shorter. He said he was in a call-box. Would I ring him back, and we could have a nice long chat, as he was free until dinner-time? He knew I would be lonely.

"I'm not lonely. I'm very happy. And I must go, darling. I've got an unexpected visitor. Yes, a visitor. He's in the garden now. You'll never guess. It's that fair man I saw at the window, the night we discovered the house. He's just called, and I'm dying to find out all about the Wynsleys—"

There was a slight disapproving pause. "You are spreading your wings."

"What do you mean, spreading my wings?"

"Oh, nothing—" But *nothing* spoke volumes.

"Don't be silly, darling. I never did like blonds. But I mustn't be impolite. Ring me tomorrow—or later tonight—"

"If I have time." He sounded chilly, and rang off.

I opened the kitchen door, went into the garden, and called: "Hello?" But as I had expected, the visitor had gone. He could hardly be expected to wait—after all, the call might have taken some time—and would have, had Derek had his way. Yet I was disappointed that he hadn't waited —disappointed out of all proportion. I had a sense of loss, as if I had been waiting for this moment, building up to something very important, and it had slipped through my fingers. I went back inside. It was absurd, I thought. A pleasantly attractive young man with a charming smile, whom I have glimpsed only a couple of times riding a black horse, and once at the window upstairs. We have greeted each other distantly and yet he's made such an impression on me that I was almost rude to poor Derek.

I spun out the rest of the day with my routine chores, never far from a window overlooking the orchard. When the dusk came, I lit the reading lamp and placed it near the window so he would know I was at home. But when darkness crept over the fields, I gave up and went upstairs to bed. I had brought a couple of paperbacks with me, but my mind kept drifting back to the Wynsleys and to Geoffrey's unfinished history.

I discovered that the branch of the family who had inherited after the disastrous fire were slightly better from a moral point of view, but the old taint in the blood persisted, the instability and eccentricity which well fitted a family cursed by the ancient murder of a priest in a sacred building. Suicides were frequent, some of them in very sad circumstances. There was Sir John, whose heir died fighting the Jacobites on the bloody field of Culloden. The two remaining sons fared little better. The second had been killed in a duel over a bad hand at cards, the third, a mere child thrown from his horse. Sir John's wife, overcome with grief, threw herself from an upstairs window, and the remaining child, a daughter—a beauty painted by Raeburn whose portrait was in Abchester Gallery—spurned marriage to look after her father.

"Her proclaimed spinsterhood was threatened by the presence of an actor who came to stay at Wynsley with Garrick, who was staging a Christmas play in the area. They fell in love, but he was married, and she was left behind at Wynsley to die of consumption, brought on perhaps by malnutrition following a broken heart. These tragic circumstances were too much for her unhappy father, who returned from her funeral and followed his wife to oblivion through the very same door, by leaping out of the upstairs window."

Poor Sir John. I wondered if there were any records of Garrick's stay. Derek would be interested in that.

That night I slept badly and awoke twice from an involved and exhausting dream whose details I could not remember. Only the moment of waking— with someone calling my name.

"Mirabel—Mirabel—"

The words were so clear that I sat up in bed, fully awake. The second time I decided that further sleep was beyond me. In the room nothing moved, only the early morning birds restlessly squabbling on the ivy-covered windowsill. I lay back, thankful that it was another day, knowing that those forgotten dreams had been troubled and unhappy. They had left a taste of sadness.

I supposed it was all the fault of my late-night reading. I remembered Garrick and that there were, according to Geoffrey Wynsley, letters and other documents in the Abchester Library. I would like to see the family portraits.

"Mad as hatters, they all were," said Mrs. Timmons when I handed the book back to her. "Be thankful, dear, that your nice Derek isn't related to any of them. You wouldn't want the Wynsley blood in your children, I can tell you. Do you think you'll like living here?" She accompanied the question with a rather odd look, I thought. When I said I loved it, she smiled. "That's good, dear. When you told me how lucky you'd been, I just wondered." She added thoughtfully, "You seem a nice sensible sort of lass, so I don't mind telling you that folk hereabouts don't care for Wynsley Manor and would gladly have seen it disappear under the motor-way."

"How dreadful! This gorgeous house. That's sacrilege."

"Gorgeous is as gorgeous does, say I. And as for sacrilege, there is a curse on the family. I'm not a superstitious woman, mind you, although I always read my horoscope and that sort of thing, but the Wynsleys and this house had a bad repu-tation. 'Wicked as Wynsley,' they used to say, to describe anyone really bad. Mind you, I've never seen or felt anything strange in this house."

"Is there something strange to see or feel?"

She put a hand to her mouth. "Now I've put my foot in it. Thought old Willis might have warned you, right at the begin-ning. Wily old devil, that he is—"

Remembering his early reluctance, then the smooth acceptance and eagerness to complete the deal, I began to see more than one chink of light where Mr. Willis was concerned. "Don't tell me we have a ghost or something, and that's why it looks like being so cheap on the market," I laughed. "Anyway, it won't put me off. I've always wanted to live in a haunted house—and according to my cousin Cora, my home in Northumberland beats this one for spooks—and I've never seen a thing. Much to my regret. I'd love to be psychic."

Mrs. Timmons eyed me sternly. "Cross your fingers, Miss Fenwick, when you speak of the devil, and never invite him across your threshold, as we say in these parts." She shook her head, smiling again. "There's no actual ghost—not that I know of. It's just that the evil of the Wynsleys seems to live on after them. They treated the tenants shamefully—real old lords of the manor. In addition to the ordinary exploitations, they had their way with any woman they fancied—and God help her parents or her man if they put up a fight. Of course, they never married these unfortunate lasses—if they were marriageable, that is. Too well-bred for peasant blood. But let me tell you, there's plenty of people in Abchester who bore a very strong resemblance to those portraits in the Gallery. Even in my mother's day, there were plenty of them around who had it. The curse of the Wynsleys, folk called it."

She pointed to the book on the table. "And *that* nice gentleman was too polite to tell one-quarter of the goings-on. Eccentric and unstable—" she sniffed. "I don't really know what all those high-falutin' words mean, but I do know they were mad —and wicked. Do you know why the villagers burnt the house down?"

"I thought it was an accident."

"Accident, my foot! It was deliberate, because the tenants couldn't take any more. The eighteenth century was a time of social upheaval, when ordinary working folk the likes of us, were beginning to realise that they were men just like the gentry, men whom their employers had turned into slaves. But they had rights of their own, the rights of every human being—" She stopped and said: "You should hear my man Charlie go on about that. He works in the factory at Abchester. Great union man he is, knows it all chapter and verse. Not that I go with him all the way—I never was radical, I think our

Queen's lovely—our Royal Family's what has kept this country respected in the eyes of the rest of the world." She paused. "Now I've lost the place—"

"Your coffee's getting cold."

"Is it? Oh, thanks. Oh, yes, there's been a lot of savage goings-on up here at the Manor. Men broken and maimed just for milord's pleasure—and his two sons, who were as bad as their old man. The Wynsleys weren't satisfied with nasty pastimes of the ordinary gentry, wrestling and cock-fighting. They wanted bigger thrills, the thought of two men murdering or maiming each other for sport, and to give them better gambling odds. And of course, the man who survived got it made worth his while. They didn't have far to search for thugs who would take on a decent man for a good prize. Not only lads, but young girls disappeared periodically and were never seen alive. Sometimes their bodies were found washed up at sea, miles away. But they weren't suicides. Some of them had terrible injuries which didn't belong to the sea. It was rumoured that they were being used in Black Mass rites in the house here and disposed of afterwards. These things were never made public by old Geoffrey in his nice family history—"

"Then how did you hear about them?"

"Oh, my Charlie's a bit of a scholar, and he had some idea of being a writer when he was young. Telling all—that sort of thing. Mind you, it never got very far, but he did have a chance to study the family papers and a lot of documents they keep in the library at Abchester. He had a theory that those secret passages could have told a thing or two as well, if any had survived when the place burned down." She put down her cup. "That must have been some blaze. There was to be a Black Mass that night, and one of the servants who was a village man and hated the Wynsleys let some of the lads in through the kitchen door here while the lord of the manor and his cronies were getting boozed up and preparing for their orgy. They crept upstairs to the bedroom and kidnapped the Wynsley daughter, who was only twelve, and fast asleep. They had a plan for her. Just before midnight the Black Mass was set up. The sacrificial victim, a pretty young girl from the village, had been abducted a day or two earlier—it must have been terrible for parents then, helpless against such monsters. All they could do, poor souls, was pray to God that they be spared the agony of a beautiful child.

"So while Wynsley and his guests got themselves into the right state of mind for the ceremony, the most trusted servant was given the job of preparing the victim. Dressing her in the great cloak and putting a golden mask on her head. It was supposed to belong to some rite in Ancient Greece and had been brought home—pinched, I suspect, by one of the travelling members of the family. In due course, when they were ready, she was led—or dragged mostly, stripped naked and strapped to the altar."

She shook her head. "My dear, I can leave the rest to your imagination—we all know enough in these modern days of telly and sex films, to spare you the details of orgies and what took place. It was, in fact, no less than communal rape. The lord of the manor, in his guise as the Devil's Anointed, took her maidenhead. His sons came next in line and had their turn, then the cronies, in order of seniority or social position. When they'd all had their bit of fun, the Devil's Anointed took out a knife and tore her heart from her living body.

"On this occasion, they hadn't quite reached the finals, as you might say, when the fire broke out in the room downstairs. They didn't know how bad it was, or how widespread, so Wynsley quickly finished off the girl, as the Devil his master was apt to be annoyed if deprived of his sacrificial cup of blood. Besides, in the confusion if she escaped—he didn't like to think of what would happen should she live to tell the tale. The body had to be got rid of. Wynsley took off the golden mask to discover that not only had he raped his virgin child, and encouraged his sons to ravish their beloved sister, but after witnessing with great delight the performance upon the altar of some twenty of his cronies, he had then brutally murdered his daughter and drunk her blood.

"It was the servant who had rescued the village lass, whom he fancied, and substituted the Wynsley girl at the last moment. He escaped from the fire and told the story, although none of the Wynsleys survived. There were stories, of course, that one son had a miraculous escape, but the others weren't so lucky—they were murdered by the villagers as they made for the stables. Anyway, the central part of the house burnt down, and for a long time stayed like that. Another Wynsley took over, a cousin from up north somewhere, but he could never rid the people of their hatred and suspicion that he was—or might turn out to be—as bad as the rest. Things went from bad to worse, just like old Geoffrey said in the book. Yes, I would love another cup of coffee, dear. Thank you."

Stirring in the sugar, she smiled at me. "Hope this gory tale doesn't put you off, Miss Fenwick, dear. After all, that part of the house is gone long since."

I suspected that in common with many middle-aged women who live rather dull but comfortable lives, she rather enjoyed telling her atrocity story to a new audience. The touch of horror was the equivalent of a shot of gin, perhaps.

"I hope I haven't put you off," she repeated. "I wouldn't want to do that."

I laughed. "It's a long time ago, isn't it —besides, I don't scare easily. My cousin Cora is much more impressionable in that respect. She's the one in the family who sees things."

"I don't suppose you know that it was my father who rebuilt the Long Gallery," she said proudly. "He was a stonemason by trade, and it was just after the War. Houses were hard to come by and this one had been empty for thirty–forty years, perhaps. There wasn't a Wynsley in sight so he decided to buy it—got it cheap, did it up. There was no window in the Long Gallery then, it was just a glorified junk hole—however, although he got a few tenants, he outsmarted himself by thinking he'd make more from renting than selling. Nobody ever stayed in it very long. That gave rise to the usual rumours, but truth be told, people didn't have so much money after the war, and not every family had two cars in the garage like now. As for commuting to London and back every day, before the motorway nobody would have thought of that. Most of the tenants were connected with the factory at Abchester, but with a poor bus service and a big house—and no shops—eventually it lay empty and derelict again."

"Did you never fancy moving in, seeing that your father owned it?"

Mrs. Timmons shuddered. "Not I— could you see my Charlie—a dyed-in-the-wool Labour man living in a place like this, reading his Karl Marx and lecturing everyone about bloated plutocrats. He'd have been the laughing-stock of the district. We know our place, Miss Fenwick, we do—and it wasn't Wynsley Manor. Not that we would have objected to the money it would have brought. However, my Dad never did have any luck. He was glad to sell it for five thousands pounds—a fortune to him, poor love, before the motorway was built and house prices went sky-high."

She paused and stared out across the apple orchard.

"Nearly ten years ago it must be, and the whole place was agog with the news that a Miss Alice Wynsley, an elderly artist lady, had been making enquiries about the Manor. She came to see Dad, and offered him what he was asking. He was amazed. She would move in immediately. She was selling her flat in London and she wanted to settle here, restore Wynsley to its former greatness. She knew all about the disreputable family, but her branch—remote cousins from Nottingham area—were honest Godfearing tradesmen, merchants and the like. She was going to put this lovely old house—as she called it—on the map again.

"We all had some doubts about that. But it was obvious that the old girl had money and plenty of it. Great furniture vans began arriving from London. She asked if she could have someone to give her a hand to get things in order, and much as I'm doing for you, dear, I offered to help. I'll never forget when I came in for the first time. I'd been used to seeing the place empty, falling to pieces, and I'd never seen furniture the like of what she was putting into the house. I don't know much about the value of antiques and quite honestly you need to be an expert, like Mr. Willis's niece Dulcie who has the shop in Abchester—and her brother, too. They're dealers and go to all the auctions at the big houses. But I could see one thing, Miss Wynsley knew what she was doing, and although the furnishings didn't add much to my ideas of comfort, she was restoring the house to its old glory, turning it into a valuable museum of antiques.

"We got along fine, Miss Wynsley and me. She let me have a free rein with the housework and she would sit upstairs in the Long Gallery hour after hour—"

"The Long Gallery?"

"Yes, she decided it was her favourite room in the house. It inspired her, she said, and she used to work there, painting. Said the light was perfect. I was always waiting for her friends coming to stay, for someone to use all these rooms she'd taken the trouble to furnish so splendidly. But no one came. Nobody but me ever entered the house. She hardly ever went into any room but the Long Gallery. Eventually she had a bed moved in there, and an electric ring and kettle. Said in the winter it was easier just to live in one room and keep it warmer. My dear, if I hadn't brought her along nourishing bowls of soup, she would have starved to death. I often thought she'd lived so long on her own, probably in one room in London—I'll bet that was what the flat amounted to—that she couldn't get used to having a great big house all around her. Wouldn't even let the Vicar's wife across the threshold. As for all those paintings, weird they were. I know what I like, but honestly, some of them gave me the horrors."

"Eccentric, was she?"

"Mad, I would have called it. At least she seemed to have inherited *that* with the family connection. As I told you, folk stayed away after poor Mrs. Brownlee's social attempts were spurned. Word got around. Then one day, it all changed. She was waiting for me when I came in.

"'Mrs. Timmons,' says she (and I wondered what I had done wrong), 'Mrs. Timmons, I want the whole house opened up, everything sparkling.'

"'Are you having visitors, Miss?'

"She laughed. 'Better than that—I'm having a permanent visitor.' And she clasped her hands together like a little girl excited by some special treat. 'Mrs. Timmons, you've been more like a friend than a servant to me—and I'm grateful— I also want you to be the first to know my wonderful news. Mrs. Timmons, I am getting married.'

"Well, you could have knocked me down with a feather. Even if she'd been young and attractive, living as she did, I would have been surprised, but she was thin and grey and plain. She looked what she was: an elderly spinster who, frankly, had never had a man in her life.

"Is the gentleman from London?" I asked, after saying how glad I was for her.

"She giggled at that and put a finger to her lips. 'As a matter of fact, no—much nearer than London. We are distantly related—he too is a Wynsley, although, alas, the family might not be prepared to recognise him. Will you do something special for me, Mrs. Timmons? Will you come with me to Abchester and help me choose a wedding dress? And of course, I must see the Vicar about making the arrangements.'

"'When is it to be?' I asked.

"'Very soon—but it is to be kept a secret. A very quiet wedding.'

"Between you and me, Miss Fenwick, I never did believe in that wedding. Mad as a hatter I thought she was—like all the rest of the Wynsleys. However, although I never had the pleasure of meeting her

116

intended, I went with her to Abchester, and was with her when she went into all the shops making the catering arrangements for the wedding. I must say I was very curious about the bridegroom, but although I tried to pump her about him, she never gave anything away.

" 'You'll find out, Mrs. Timmons, and everyone else in Wynsley and Abchester too, who have been laughing at me, thinking I was a mad old maid, are going to be so surprised when I do the laughing for a change.'

"As you might imagine, she was the sensation of Abchester, with her old-fashioned tweed coat, her down-at-heel shoes, her ancient felt hat—and always with a portfolio of paintings under her arm, scuttling from one shop to another.

"And who was this Wynsley chap she talked about?

"That was a poser, and no one could guess the answer. Folk decided he must be from London or Nottingham and she was being coy, since all the Wynsleys in these parts had been sleeping peacefully—or not so peacefully, perhaps—in their graves for more than a hundred years. However, people from around about were curious, but although they kept a lookout for some strange man who might be visiting, nobody ever saw her with anyone— although there were those ready to swear she was always roaming about near the house, talking to herself. Mad she was, poor old thing. Worst of all was when she tried to get the Vicar to fix the ceremony and refused to give the bridegroom's name. Wanted it to be a surprise, she insisted. A surprise for whom, demanded Mr. Brownlee, pointing out that the wedding would not be legal unless the banns were called and the registrar at Abchester also liked to be informed. She was absolutely furious, came back to the house here snorting with fury and almost in tears. The Vicar had been cross and she had lost her temper. I gave her a strong cup of coffee, tried to soothe her down. I was sorry for the poor demented soul, raving she was, suffering from hallucinations. That afternoon I went into Abchester specially to see Dulcie Willis who had got friendly with her because of their shared interest in antiques. She'd been coming over at weekends when the shop was closed and staying—the only guest I'd known Miss Wynsley ever to have in the house. She never came when I was there, of course." The accompanying sniff of disapproval indicated that Mrs. Timmons had been ousted from her role of confidante in Miss Wynsley's life by Miss Willis. I guessed it was curiosity that had prompted the visit to the antique shop, as she continued.

"When I mentioned the wedding and how anxious and worried I was, she shut up like a clam and said it was really none of our business and she wasn't prepared to discuss Miss Wynsley's affairs with anyone —even if she knew all about it, which she didn't. 'Her behaviour is as much a mystery to me as to the rest of Abchester.'"

Again the sniff of outrage. "A very uppity thing is our Miss Willis. They've always been a bit above themselves, she and her young brother. However, she promised to look in, by all means, later when Shane returned from an auction up north and could take over the shop. And she would certainly go to Wynsley as she'd arranged with Miss Wynsley on her usual half-day closing. She would see what she could do.

"But by Thursday afternoon, poor Miss Wynsley was beyond anyone's help. One of the farmers going past with his tractor saw the window of the Long Gallery lying wide open, banging in the wind. He looked over the wall and saw her in a heap under the balcony. She'd been dead for hours."

Mrs. Timmons shook her head sadly. "The inquest decided it was accidental death. The doctor said she had high blood pressure and was subject to dizzy spells. She had probably opened the window for fresh air, and fallen out."

Mrs. Timmons frowned and I asked: "Do you think that was what happened?"

"I'd like to, Miss Fenwick. Really I would. I'd prefer not to think the poor soul had a sudden lucid spell in her madness and realised her romantic dream of a husband and a wedding was all a lot of rubbish. Imagine knowing she would have to face everyone—that they would all be laughing at her. I would prefer to think that she died happy, in a quick accident, believing to the end that she was loved by someone."

"Her ending was certainly in keeping with the family tradition. They seemed to have a nasty habit of falling out of windows."

"Indeed they did." Mrs. Timmons tapped Geoffrey Wynsley's book. "D'you know, there was only one of them I had the slightest sympathy for. And that was poor Sir John—"

"The one who lost all his family one after another—poor man."

"Small wonder he jumped out of the window to end it all. No one could blame him for that. Incidentally, one of Dad's tenants years ago had a little lass who was, well, a bit peculiar. Funny things happened when she was in the house, and she swore that she'd seen Sir John—met him on the stairs and heard him calling for his beloved lost daughter. The little girl's mother believed every word of it. Mind you, I think she would have been cured by a smacked bottom. However, she upset her brothers and sisters so much by her goings-on that they moved into another house in Abchester."

Mrs. Timmons smiled. "And that is the only haunting I've ever heard about. I've heard of people being uncomfortable, but never anything you could describe as a ghost." She leaned over and patted my hand. "And I wouldn't be telling you about it, if you were one prone to see things—ghosts, and all that sort of nonsense, I mean. I do think that a lot of it is just in people's imagination and they want to scare other more sensible folk with their stories—do it all for effect."

As I helped her put away the dishes, she said: "By the way, there's a lovely memorial to Sir John's daughter in the graveyard—a marble figure of her playing with her favourite cat. Some famous sculptor did it for Sir John in her lifetime, and when she died, he asked that it be her gravestone. Sad it was when you remember her story, that actor letting her down so badly—typical. Of those days," she added hastily. "Actors are more like ordinary decent people nowadays, like your lovely Derek. It's the telly really that has improved them, made them more like real people."

I was glad she didn't know some of the

horrendous inside stories that were common knowlege in the studios, bless her dear innocent heart. And I shared a moment's thought for my lovely Derek, as she called him, and my cousin, wondering whether they were playing me false.

"Do look out for the monument, and her picture is in the Gallery at Abchester, too. Lovely girl she was, long fair hair—just like your own. Come to think of it, you should be particularly interested in her." She smiled at me, head on one side. "Bet you can't guess what her name was."

A jet screamed overhead. I waited until the silence came back, and in a voice that sounded unnecessarily loud, asked: "It wasn't Mirabel, by any chance—was it?"

She nodded eagerly. "Now, isn't that a coincidence. Such an unusual name. I like the nice old-fashioned ones myself. I was just saying to my daughter, I hope when the new baby arrives they choose a *sensible* name—"

I wasn't listening to her anymore.

Mirabel—Mirabel. I was remembering that I had heard my name called on two occasions and that the second time—on that morning—it had been distinct enough to awaken me from a deep sleep.

Suddenly it seemed very important to remember what I had been dreaming about that had left its taste of sadness. I was certain that it had something to do with this house, that I had been unhappy, but worse than that, I had, in my dream, been in considerable danger from forces within the empty house.

6

I KNEW beyond any shadow of doubt that I had heard my name called in the house.

Mirabel—Mirabel.

Without Mrs. Timmons' presence the silence was suddenly oppressive, like a stern questioner expecting an answer.

She had departed full of good cheer, unaware of the seeds of fear her lurid tales of the wicked Wynsleys had sown in my quiet kitchen. Kindly and honest, her intention had never been to scare. She would have been appalled at the idea, but since I had scornfully rejected any belief in the supernatural, she had assumed I was of the same persuasion as herself: solid, unimaginative, practical. She had never supposed for an instant that about the business of ghosts, there are degrees of terror.

Before Mrs. Timmons' revelations, I had been prepared to dismiss the voice calling "Mirabel" as part of my allergy—

125

noises in the head brought about by excessive sneezing seemed the logical explanation. Since Mrs. Timmons' visit, I could no longer take refuge in such allowance or excuse. She had put a face to my mysterious voice. A face and a body—that of poor, ill-fated Sir John.

I suppose I should have been grateful that matters were no worse than that. If it is possible also to have degrees of gratitude for hauntings, then I should have had a sense of relief that I was the object of earthly interest to a benign but demented Wynsley on a quest for the lost daughter who bore my name, rather than Hellfire Wynsley returned on a quest for young ladies for his beastly Black Mass rites.

At that moment, I had very little desire to go upstairs and continue my domestic activities of cleaning and lining those dark bedroom cupboards and cavernous wardrobes with their lurking spider population. I found myself moving silently, almost on tiptoe, listening—hearing in every normal creak of an ancient house the sound of a stealthy footfall. Somewhere, unseen, a trapped insect buzzed furiously, seeking escape.

I felt a certain sympathy with it as I opened the kitchen door and leaned against the wall, glad of the normality of sunlight—normality and cleansing grace. From the lane beyond the orchard came the welcome sound of an approaching tractor. I watched it progressing steadily toward the house, scattering tall grasses in a wild, reaping movement. Large and bright yellow, big of wheel and shining blade, it looked like some monster from a science fiction serial, as much an anachronism in this quiet countryside as the Elizabethan manor house of Wynsley.

Its driver had observed me, and stopped by the orchard gate.

"Hello there!"

A man's voice, and for a heart-stopping moment, a glimpse of yellow hair under a cap. I hurried across the orchard, but it wasn't my stranger. A lad of fourteen or so sat at the wheel.

"Hello, missus. Ours is the farm over yonder, and my da thought you'd like the lane here kept clear. Bit overgrown it is, but you'd find it quicker to the village—and the Abchester bus—than round by the Vicarage. Folk who lived here before

127

always used this way." I thanked him, and he grinned: "You'll be able to drive a car along, no trouble—bit rocky, that's all. No extra work, missus—it's an easy matter to work our way down here when we're cutting hay in the next field."

After he'd gone, the silence came back. I looked at the house and decided I needed a change of scene. I would go into Abchester, to the library and Art Gallery. I was suddenly lonely for Derek—and Cora —and wished I was with them in London.

I went inside, gathered together the things I would need, and hurried down the lane, which was at least negotiable, but would give Derek a fit trying to bring his nice Porsche Carrera through such an ordeal. With ten seconds to spare, I was just in time to see the Abchester bus flee past. I looked at my timetable. There wasn't another until 4:30, which made my journey futile. I decided to treat myself to afternoon tea at the Wynsley Arms, instead.

I was greeted like an old friend, and Mrs. Timmons rushed out from the kitchen and whispered: "What would you like to drink?" When I said, "Not at this time of day," she replied: "Go on—it's on the house. To celebrate my first grand-child. Betty got a little lad and they're both doing fine—and born on Abchester's gala day of the year!"

I had forgotten about the Flower Festival. "Good job you didn't get the bus, dear. You'd have found all the shops closed and everyone preparing for the great event. Now what'll you have to drink?"

The baby's health was duly drunk and I forgot the idea of afternoon tea and sand-wiches when the doors opened and a crowd of school children rushed in with armsful of garlands. "They've come to decorate for this evening," said Mrs. Timmons. "Righto—you lot—put them down over there. Yes, I'll tell you what has to be done. Can't you see I'm busy at the moment?"

The drink had been generous in every sense of the word. I decided to go to Abchester for the Festival. If I could perhaps hint to the Brownlees they might even offer me a lift. Mr. Brownlee was busy in his garden.

"Oh, hello, my dear—what can I do for you? Or are you just passing by?"

"Actually, I thought I might give Mrs. Brownlee a hand with the children's costumes. She was telling me about them yesterday—for the Festival."

"Oh, my dear, you've just missed her. She's away round the farms to distribute them—car packed to the roof. What a pity. I'm sure she would have loved to have your assistance—how very kind."

Feeling hypocritical, because the lift to Abchester had been my main reason for the offer, I told him about the missed bus.

"I would have taken you like a shot. But Margaret has the car and I usually wait here at the Wynsley Arms. Traditionally, I greet the arrival of the procession. Besides, all the crowds at Abchester aren't very good for me. Why don't you stay at the Arms too—have a ringside seat until bedlam descends upon us?" I thought that would be a good idea. "How did you enjoy Geoffrey's little book?"

"Very much," I said, although I felt that, in view of my present enlightenment about Sir John Wynsley, *enjoy* was a poor word.

On my way back to the house, I decided to inspect the monumental tomb of Miss Mirabel Wynsley. It wasn't difficult to find —tall and imposing and rather ugly. It was pathetic, too, I thought, standing on the pebbly path staring up at the inscription which said only: "For my well-beloved daughter Mirabel."

I stood there for a long time, hoping, I think, that it would arouse some emotion, some feeling of kinship. I felt nothing at all, and was grateful for that—at least Sir John's ghost didn't hover near the marble statue.

As soon as I opened the kitchen door, I knew that I was still afraid, that I was still in a state of suspenseful alertness. I had to go upstairs and change into something suitable for the evening's activities, but I dreaded the staircase, the bedroom, the shadow of the Long Gallery waiting at the end of the corridor. If I opened those locked doors, what might I find?

"Take a grip of yourself, Mab." I could almost hear Derek's sharp rejoinder. "Pull yourself together." The words he used when I did something silly in the car. Oh, dear God, I wish you were here, Derek—

Well, he's not here, silly, and you have only yourself to blame. You chose to live here. You wanted this house. And now you've got it and you have to stay here, so you might as well get to grips with the situation and make the best of it. You could make a start by turning on the radio —loud—that should keep any whispers at bay.

I took the transistor with me from room to room, listening with determination rather than enjoyment to its loud, insidious blare. It certainly did keep the shadows at bay. Not even poor Sir John on the prowl could have competed with the twentieth century made manifest at its vulgar, strident worst.

I put on my prettiest dress, made up my face carefully, and set out for the Flower Festival. I had reached the orchard gate when I heard the phone ringing in the kitchen and knew it was Derek. I raced back, but by the time I had unlocked the door and put my hand on the receiver, it went dead.

I was furious—and I knew Derek would be too. I felt frustrated and miserable, wishing there were some way I could contact him apart from the studio. I waited around for ten minutes, hoping he would phone again, and then, closing the door behind me, went down to Wynsley.

I was just in time for the arrival of the procession. The first of the flower floats, a huge crown made of garlands, had as its "jewel" a rather dazzling lady dressed as Queen Elizabeth herself. This, I learned, had won the first prize. She was followed by her courtiers in their Tudor costumes, and as I watched them descend on the Wynsley Arms, I felt an odd sense of *déjá vu*. All this had been happening year after year for nearly four hundred years, this tiny vignette of life unchanged, perhaps only suspended during wars and social upheavals. This ancient revival of a pagan ritual was the very basis of life at Wynsley.

The other floats were scarcely less magnificent, and the judges must have had a hard time of it. The pages of history, the great events, were all there. The only modern note was struck by the Children's Festival, with their themes from television serials, nursery rhymes and the like. It was all very touching, and pretty, too.

"Yes, I'm so glad I didn't miss it," I

told Mrs. Timmons, who was overseeing with Mrs. Brownlee the departure of those of tender years who couldn't be admitted to licensed premises.

"There's lemonade and cakes laid out for them along at the scout hut next to the garage."

I noticed that the Vicar and his wife weren't among the teetotallers who departed with the youngsters and I chatted to Mr. Brownlee, happily ensconced behind a large pot of draught beer, while his wife toyed with a more ladylike sherry in keeping with the Vicarage image.

"Queen Elizabeth" pushed her way through the crowd and they both sprang up to greet her, the Vicar insisting she take his seat beside me and rushing off to order her a gin and tonic.

"That's better," she said. "What a terrible crush! It gets worse each year, don't you think, Margaret?" she added to Mrs. Brownlee.

"I expect there are fewer occasions now for people to have the chance to dress up. Oh, Miss Fenwick—you haven't met Dulcie Willis, have you?"

"Queen Elizabeth" shook my hand

"I'm so glad to meet you—welcome to Wynsley." When I congratulated her on winning and on her magnificent dress, she looked very pleased. "I've never entered a float before. This is the first time."

"Dulcie is usually too busy organising everyone else in Abchester," said Margaret, giving her a fond glance.

"I don't know whether I'd call it that or not."

"Go along with you, my dear—you're at everyone's beck and call." Mrs. Brownlee turned to me and said: "I don't know how she manages it, especially with the antique shop as well. Giving talks to evening classes—Dulcie is an expert on old furniture, you know—rushing up and down to London—"

"Margaret dear, do spare my blushes. You'll terrify poor Miss Fenwick, making me out such a paragon." She turned to me, smiling. "It's really more of an obsession than a hobby. I just adore the past—and history. I'm not impressed by this modern age at all, and I do want to see the past kept alive here at Wynsley." She paused and said: "I do envy you

Wynsley Manor. I hear you're the new owner."

I explained about the absent Wynsley and that if he could be found and he was willing to sell, Derek and I would be interested.

"I never met him," said Dulcie, "although Miss Wynsley mentioned him from time to time."

This was the opening I had been waiting for. "You knew Miss Wynsley quite well, didn't you?"

At that moment, a pot of beer shot across the table, followed by a large young man, who steadied himself and apologised drunkenly, offering to mop up and producing a large hankie. He managed to spread the disaster even further as it poured over the edges of the table and we all sprang to our feet. One of the bartenders arrived on the scene, and Dulcie Willis rushed off into the cloakroom rather wildly, saying:

"It's only a borrowed dress—I do hope it doesn't leave a stain."

Mrs. Brownlee accompanied her and I was alone for a moment and then

136

surrounded by a slightly tipsy group of lads, all offering to buy me drinks.

One of them threw a garland around my neck. Another whispered: "And what's your name, my pretty dear?" A third said: "You from Abchester?" A fourth added: "She's never from Abchester—I'd never have forgotten meeting you, honey." "Stranger, are you?" asked his companion. "Down for the gala?"

Mrs. Timmons witnessed our progress through the throng to the bar, and was perhaps aware of my pleading glance for rescue. She bustled forward and said: "Don't you lot harass Miss Fenwick."

"Why not?"

"Because she's spoken for, that's why not."

"And who's the lucky man, Timmy— anyone we know?"

"*Mrs. Timmons* to you, Josh White." And before I could stop her—I should have recognised that she had also been celebrating and was therefore likely to be more garrulous than usual—she had launched into my approaching marriage to Derek Wynsley. "Yes," she ended triumphantly, "Miss Fenwick's going to be the future Lady Amyas Symon."

Most of them had seen the series and were delighted to chat with someone vicariously connected with what they considered the glamorous world of television. They were nice lads, all of them, eager to be friendly. Apart from refusing drinks, which they persisted in buying, so that I had a small but imposing array of glasses on my corner of the table, somewhat awash with spilt beer, I found I was rather enjoying being the centre of attraction. It seemed a long time since I had enjoyed male flattery, and when Mr. Brownlee peered over their heads, eyebrows raised indicating: *Do you want to escape?* I shook my head. I was happy in the silly badinage and they found that I could give as good as I got.

"Time, gentlemen, please. Drink up now, ladies and gentlemen. Time *please*." In the traditional manner of the English pub, everyone delayed until the last possible moment, and finally, I am ashamed to say, I was the last to leave, with two of my remaining companions insisting that they see me home.

And so I walked up the dusky lane arm-in-arm with Josh White and his mate Dave. As we approached the house, I wondered what Sir John—if he was lurking about searching for Mirabel—made of the fascinating trio. Two Elizabethan courtiers, their costumes and ruffs a bit the worst for wear, and a girl with long straight hair in a dress that had not yet been invented in his age. I could be flippant about Sir John and the other ghosts of Wynsley from this world of mine. In this twentieth century I could look over at the house, brooding and dark, its windows unlit, and say:

"I don't believe in ghosts. You are all dead—with the past. None of you can harm me."

I was aware of Josh and Dave silently watching the house.

"How do you like living at the Manor, then?"

"Very much."

They eyed it doubtfully. "Bit big, isn't it—I mean, all those rooms," said Josh.

"We used to play in it when it was empty—years ago, when we were kids. That was before Miss Wynsley's time."

"Yes. We used to play spooky games and nearly frighten each other to death. Up and down those stairs, hiding in cupboards—what fun it was!"

"I suppose it's very grand now—not a bit like it was."

The wistful tones were irresistible. They were also exactly what I needed. Someone young and cheerful to come into the house with me and dispel the gloom my own imagination had created. There was nothing wrong with the house. I had let myself be convinced of Sir John, just because Mrs. Timmons had told me about his daughter. Mirabel wasn't a specially unusual name—I'd almost certainly heard it on the radio, and imagined the rest.

"Would you like to see it now?" I asked. "Come in and have coffee."

With two nice, ordinary lads at my side, I climbed the stairs and opened all the doors, including the Long Gallery, which they pronounced as a "funny sort of room. What would anyone want with a place like that?"

I discovered that they were farmhands from Abchester way. They both lived in little old-fashioned cottages and had never

seen places like this "except on the telly."
I was glad of their loud voices, their
giggling appreciation of four-poster beds
and their laughter and mock terror at
sleeping in such vast caverns of bedrooms.
I was glad of their loud footsteps on the
stairs and switched on the radio when
we went back to the kitchen, glad of my
restoration to my own time.

They left at midnight and as I waved
them goodnight, promising to have a drink
with them later in the week if Derek
hadn't returned, the orchard was full of
moonlight.

"Lovely evening, isn't it? It's just like
daylight!"

It was, too. I watched them disappear
through the gate and went back into the
house. There was dance music on the radio
and as I gathered together the cups and
plates and washed them, I sang in my very
indifferent voice. I felt happy—I had
made two new friends. And I felt safe—
tomorrow was a new day, and I had
learned a lesson. In the future I would not
be quite so impressionable. I had almost
persuaded myself that Wynsley Manor was
haunted. If it hadn't been for Josh and

Dave, and their very twentieth-century sanity, I would have been terrified to come back here on my own tonight.

The very idea! At that moment I looked out the window and saw a figure at the orchard gate.

He was walking toward the house alone, his cloak swinging from his shoulders. The light was strong enough for me to see that he was wearing Tudor dress. I felt a moment's shocked indignation at his stealthy approach, followed by a sense of anger and betrayal.

My late night caller was either Josh or Dave, who for some reason of his own— alas, a reason that wasn't particularly hard to guess—had decided to return and start a party of quite a different nature.

I was so disappointed. They'd seemed such nice, straightforward lads. Yet, I supposed, one never could be certain. After all, I *had* let them pick me up in a pub and buy me drinks. Presumably they had come to certain conclusions. It fitted a pattern of behaviour they associated with girls of their acquaintance—that I was a different kind of girl hadn't occurred to them, any more than telling frightening tales of the Wynsleys had seemed wrong to Mrs. Timmons.

Well, Josh—or Dave—you are in for a surprise! I opened the door, ready to be cold and very distant. It never occurred to me that I would have been safer to have locked the door instead.

There was no one outside.

At least that was my first impression. I couldn't see anyone. I called, "Is that you, Josh—Dave—hello? Did you forget something?"

No one answered me, and completely mystified and afraid, I was about to go in and lock the door when I saw him leaning against a tree in the orchard, watching me. He was near enough for me to recognise him—neither Josh nor Dave, but my blond stranger.

"Hello—again." I shouted. There was only twenty feet or so between me where I stood at the kitchen door and him by the apple tree. But shyness overcame me. Suddenly the moves had to come from him. I remembered how I had raced towards him last night when the phone had rung. I didn't want to look too eager. I leaned against the door and waited.

I saw him bow, a gesture out-of-date but charming and very much more natural in that Tudor dress than any of Derek's studio-created actions.

"Hello, I do hope I'm not intruding—"

"Of course not." (Past midnight? Really, Mab, you must be joking!) "I mean—I was just going to bed—I've been at the Flower Festival—Came home with a couple of friends—" (For heaven's sake —*do* try to sound natural and relaxed.)

"I saw you there."

"I didn't see you."

"Oh, I was there." (Well, that's obvious enough from the costume he's wearing.) He was looking at the house, his face pale in the moonlight, expressionless. "So you're the new tenant—how do you like living here?"

"Very much indeed. It's a beautiful house, isn't it?"

"I'm glad you like it. You can't imagine what it was like once upon a time. Far grander than this. This is a mere fragment of its former glory."

"I know. As a matter of fact, I've just been reading a family history."

"Geoffrey's, I suppose. That man has

much to answer for. He never told half the truth about it. How could he, anyway? *He* had no imagination." He paused, and I said:

"Do you know Mrs. Timmons?"

"Everyone knows Mrs. Timmons."

"She told me a lot of the things that weren't in the history book. About the Wynsleys."

He laughed, throwing back his head. Silent laughter, I thought, darkening only the sockets of his eyes and making the wide mouth a black cavern. "Mrs. Timmons is a fool. She can think of nothing but the people. The people aren't important. They were just passing shades, no more important than the swallows who build their nests, spend a summer breeding young, quarrelling, and then vanish without a trace. The Wynsleys weren't the important factor in the history at all—the house here, which has endured through so many centuries, survived so many of its owners' follies, is the important part to remember."

It was quite a speech. "It depends on whether you consider things more important than people."

"Some things are. I would sacrifice a great many of the world's population to keep its treasure intact."

"Aren't you forgetting that man made most of those treasures?"

He looked at me, smiling and pleased, but I knew I had scored a point. But the argument—the test—was over. In some subtle way, the relationship had changed, as he continued:

"Before the fire—can you imagine the scene before you? The house with its hundred rooms lit by thousands of candles, with carriages rolling up the drive —over there and long a wilderness of weeds. There were great ornate gates too, and they took them away during the war and turned them into bullets. Bullets— those gates had been famous for centuries, and they melted them down. Barbarians, the lot of them."

"I seem to have read somewhere that bullets were needed if we were not to be overrun by barbarians. England's just a little island—"

"England or the Nazis—not much to choose between them now. Wars to end wars usually only mean the end of another epoch of civilisation. The Wynsleys knew all about that, too. In the library, they had every shelf packed with the cream of the world's great literature. In days when few men read or collected books, philosophers came from far and wide, privileged to see the Wynsley library."

"What happened to them?"

"Man again, in his ignorance. Some fool of a Victorian decided that the vast collection of eroticism from Persia and India offended against morality. Some unsuspecting child or innocent virgin might by accident look on the illustrations and be sullied forever. They took them out to the orchard here—and—burned—them."

For once I could understand his ferocity. "The prudery of the Victorians was beyond belief, sometimes."

He nodded. "And yet it was a time of enlightenment, of great progress—it had a certain nobility and enchantment. The beginning of the emergence of man, the exploration of the unconscious, the unseen. Men were soon to realise that there were more things in this world than could be seen with their own eyes, or heard with their own ears. Man was on the

147

threshold of discovering that besides the senses he had taken for granted, he had been given and had lost an extra one, the sixth sense—and by regaining it, all knowledge, all truth would be his for the taking. He could be master of the entire universe. Many of the first conversations about extra-sensory perception, about parapsychology, were begun here in Wynsley."

A vision of Sir John floated into my mind, and as if he could read the thought he said: "The eighteenth-century Wynsleys were vulgarians, ignorant and foolish. It was up to the Victorians to carry on the great tradition of the Elizabethans. Think of it, on summer nights like this, with the spinet playing in the drawing-room, the laughter drifting out to us from the open windows. And wine, wine sparkling like blood as the greatest wits and the greatest beauties of the day gathered to sup together at Wynsley. Think of that—" He threw back his head and laughed again, and I shivered, not from cold but because for a moment I fancied those windows before us were filled with the light of a bygone age. But suddenly, instead of being charming, it was sinster, frightening—

"You paint a fascinating picture," I said.

"There are still ways of getting back," he said.

"Back?"

"Yes, into the past." He looked at me. "It is easy, once you find the path."

"I would be afraid."

"Afraid?"

"Yes, in case I wouldn't return to the present."

He was smiling. "Maybe you wouldn't want to return to the present. Have you ever thought of that?" He paused. "This house has always seemed part of me, although I've never lived in it."

"Yes, I felt that way too—the moment I set eyes on it."

He seemed pleased. "May I know your name?"

"Mirabel—Mirabel Fenwick. My friends call me Mab."

"Mab?" He shrugged. "No—I don't like Mab. Mirabel." He repeated it softly. "A lovely name. I do hate these modern names," and for the first time in my life

Mirabel ceased to suggest the dairy farm and the prize cow.

"Perhaps you would like to come inside some time when you're passing and have a look at the house. I'm afraid most of the furniture is Victorian—a few antiques, not many. Not really in period anymore, I'm afraid."

"I would like to come—to see you. But I know the house very well. I've been in there many times."

"You live near here?"

He pointed a vague hand in the direction of Abchester. "Quite near. May I see you again, Mirabel?"

"Of course. We're on the phone—my fiancé Derek will be back soon from London—he'd love to meet you." (Oh, how false you are, Mab—you know having him meet Derek is the last thing in the world you want to happen!)

He waved aside my clumsy hints about Derek. "Would tomorrow evening be too soon?"

"That would be splendid—come and have a meal with me, about eight—I loath eating alone." (Now you've gone and done it, Mab Fenwick. What do you think

you're playing at? The man's a stranger—
a nice-looking one—but he could be
anyone—you're crazy—)

He bowed. "I shall be delighted," and
he moved out of the shadows, the moonlight turning his hair to silver. He was
smiling as he walked toward where I
stood. He's going to embrace me—I know
it. I closed my eyes, waiting—

When I opened them he was watching
me gravely, an arm's-length away. "You
are very lovely, Mirabel," he said gently.

A wind had arisen from nowhere,
shaking my moon-lit dream world, turning
it into a backdrop from an indifferent
musical comedy. But *he* seemed to glide
on the wind, it lifted the edges of his cloak
as if he were being carried on swift dark
wings toward the orchard gate.

He was going away—I was losing him.
(You'll see him again tomorrow, said
conscience, more fool you—and you don't
even know his name—)

Of course I didn't. I had forgotten to
ask as he eulogised over mine.

"What's your name?" I shouted.

He was on the other side of the gate,
and turning, he held up his hand, the

rising wind tearing at his cloak, his hair, as if in some frenzy it wanted to rush him away from me.

"Name—" he shouted, and the rest was lost in the creaking branches of the apple trees between us. A cloud slipped across the moon and he vanished from my sight.

7

I SLEPT badly that night, not out of fear, but excitement. I lay in my great bed, staring at the window and planning the evening ahead. Every time the clock struck, I thought with joy—one hour less, one hour nearer to our next meeting. I thought about the meal I would serve with apparent casualness, but planned it to the last detail. I didn't know his taste in food and I would take Derek's advice when we entertained strangers.

"Make it plain but good—something you're sure of that won't go wrong at the last moment. Never try out a new recipe, however tempting."

A sirloin roast, with baked potatoes, some interesting vegetables with sauces, Yorkshire pudding. Begin with iced melon, and with the cheesecake that was my own speciality. I had gin, whisky, martini—thank goodness Derek had invested in some bottles of wine our first evening here—and I had found myself unconsciously planning the menu that Derek loved most. Add candlelight to wine, soft music . . .

At nine o'clock that morning I hurried down the lane with my shopping list. As the bus for Abchester sped through the two miles which separated it from Wynsley, it stopped for the farm wives, the school children, making me remember that all this land had once been the property of the manor, its vast estate. The charming old stone cottages had been occupied by the tenants, paying their rents to the lord. Some of the farm workers' cottages were as old as Wynsley itself, and much more elegant and picturesque than those I associated with their equivalent in the north. Many of them had lost all connection with the farming community and would be far beyond the reach of the agricultural workers for whom they had originally been intended. Most were now in the hands of rich businessmen who could afford the luxury of commuting to London each day.

My second impression of Abchester was no improvement on the first brief visit with Derek when we had called upon Mr.

Willis and rented Wynsley Manor. Abchester's rose-red setting, so pretty tempered by distance as seen from the ruined tower about the manor, was an ugly reality, a sprawl of red-brick streets sloping to the river. A few factory chimneys, one long main street full of parked cars and an assortment of shops, ancient and modern, but none worthy of a second glance for their architecture's sake.

Abchester had been built close to the industrial revolution in the hope that business and factories would turn it into a boom town. Now the local factories stood empty and derelict, still pathetically waiting for the days of prosperity that had passed the sleepy town long ago. The houses too, those built with an eye to big business by Victorians with large families, crouched behind high hedges, all turreted and many-windowed, a study in red brick dilapidation and a lesson in the perfect heights to which bad taste in architecture could, with time and money to burn, arise. Some brave souls with kind hearts had tried to salvage the mediocre best of Abchester and turn it into a vast dormitory. There was a railway station, and the London train stopped at Abchester on request. The other inhabitants had not been so fortunate in this piece of rural England at its worst and from the poky hovels which rich men had thought good enough for their wretched employees a hundred and fifty years ago, travelled to the vast motor works twelve miles away by bus and motorbike.

As I dashed from shop to shop, the rain began, and completing my purchases as quickly as possible, I found the Art Gallery, Museum and Library all housed under one roof in a vast Victorian building next to the Town Hall which would have unhesitatingly carried off first prize in an architectural monstrosity competition. If possible, its mausoleum of an interior was only one degree worse than its outside, an uninspired decor overburdened by replicas of famous statues from ancient Greece. In the Museum, the main exhibits were a weary collection of Egyptology—two mummies in decaying bandages—and Natural History, some dusty animals whose fur had long since fallen to the ravages of mange. There were some regional "finds." Roman and Saxon fragments of pottery, some stones from excavations on the site of Wynsley Priory.

"Wynsley Collection." I followed the arrow to a room whose dark walls were lined with even darker family portraits. Pale faces stared out of the gloom of dingy oil paintings. Below them, a few early English chairs, their carving heavily varnished, almost obliterating the worn initials of the Tudor owners. The centre of the room was occupied by a large glass case containing old spectacles, snuff boxes, miniatures, fans and patch boxes, once the property of the Wynsley family. One lonely Elizabethan lady's shoe and a pair of Victorian lady's boots, so tiny it seemed unbelievable that a fully grown woman had ever worn them.

On the wall and occupying the place of honour, resting on red velvet in an ancient gold frame, was a faded leather gauntlet, the kind used by ladies for falconry. On the ornately embroidered cuff were the initials "A.B." woven in seed pearls.

So this was Anne Boleyn's gift to her kind host at Wynsley. As I looked at it, I again marvelled at the size of our hands and feet compared with those of our female ancestors. The glove had been made for a tiny hand with long slender fingers, scarcely larger than a child's.

Truth to tell, I had never thought much about Anne Boleyn until that moment, when I saw the glove and realised the tiny childlike hands of its owner. That little glove made her, for me, a real person. It carried her tragedy into the present and made her death even more cruel and unnecessary than history books or films had ever implied. I saw Henry the Eighth, rough and red-eyed, holding it in his great hands, driven to the desperation of divorcing poor Catherine of Aragon because of his lust for Anne. And I wondered again about the love that had him rushing to Wynsley to dally with her, being held at arm's-length until he agreed to her terms of marriage. I saw him frustrated, mad with desire, in the ruined tower of Wynsley, coaxing her—a great king down on his knees, begging his subject for what was any lover's right. And I remembered that love once gratified had turned to boredom, then to a hatred strong enough to bring her to death under the executioner's axe.

Poor little Anne, trying in vain to hold her wild, randy husband who could give her all the jewels of England but couldn't put a healthy male child in her womb. Such are the misfortunes of kings and great dynasties with all to win or lose on the gamble of a male heir. The Wynsleys, too, had suffered, and all they had left to posterity were a few and dusty mementos of their dynasty, the treasures of the great house diminished to the contents of a glass case in the regional museum and a roomful of portraits.

I turned my attention to them. A painting of the house as it had been, referred to in Geoffrey's book. Very grand and fanciful, all opal shades with a foreground of diminutive figures with their horses and dogs, their children playing— a pretty pastoral of a scene that had never existed, I was sure, outside the artist's imagination. Wynsley Tower was much painted, a favourite subject with the ladies of thc family, all of whom were addicted to rather timorous water-colours. Except for Alice Wynsley, several of whose original studies in oil had been "kindly donated to this collection by the artist."

The family portraits were mostly of the Victorian era, and rather dull. Presumably the colourful, early Wynsleys and in particular the "wicked" ones had more important matters to engage their attention than sitting for tedious portraits. I suppose that any from that time would have perished in the fire.

I moved on, found myself facing a Raeburn, surely the most valuable asset of the Museum. "Mirabel Wynsley, 1723–48." I had imagined she would be older, having been described as a spinster. The pale and tragic face, the formalised hair style certainly suggested a greater age than twenty-five. I had not realised that she was my own age when she died, since I still considered myself young. However, where marriageable years began at fifteen, I presumed that if one had been awaiting a husband unsuccessfully for ten years, with a life expectancy of less than fifty, one might reasonably be expected to regard arrival at the quarter-century as signifying middle-age when most of one's contemporaries were already mothers of young families.

I was considerably relieved to see that

name, age and hair colour were all I shared with Mirabel Wynsley, and that there was no striking resemblance. It was consoling to realise that as I was quite unlike his daughter, Sir John's "haunting" could now be relegated to the realm of coincidence—a name on the radio, and, more unromantic, noises in the head brought about by a severe attack of hay fever.

I was getting more interested now. It was fun seeing all these old pictures, forming some idea of the people who had inhabited the manor before me. I was glad I had taken the trouble to come to the Museum.

I stopped dead in my tracks, my heart beating uncomfortably loud. There before me, smiling and serene, was a face I recognised.

"Portrait of a Tudor Gentleman. Artist Unknown." A small plaque underneath stated: "This portrait was found in the house during restoration and is believed to be Sir Robert Wynsley, friend of Henry the Eighth, painted by a pupil of Hans Holbein."

Pale hair, deep-set blue eyes—it was the face of my midnight visitor, the horseman who had ridden past the orchard, the man I had seen leaning out of the window the evening I first saw Wynsley Manor.

The room seemed to have darkened around me, the atmosphere chilled as if the temperature had suddenly dropped. I was conscious of being alone and menaced by all that remained of the Wynsleys, this room of portraits and possessions. It was as if they resented my life when they were dead and dust, and as if their ghosts had gathered in the dark shadows of the room, their spectral hands, shattering the glass, were reaching out to touch me.

I turned and fled, relieved by the noise my footsteps made, glad to escape from that world of the past. At the information desk, I gathered my shopping bag and raincoat and fled into the dreariness of Abchester, no longer resenting that it wasn't beautiful and old, but grateful for the mundane shops, the cars and buses, the housewives with their headscarves and umbrellas, the small children.

I hurried toward the bus station. When I got back to Wynsley Manor, I must get in touch with Derek—or Cora. If I phoned the studio, I should be able to find them.

Perhaps I could take an afternoon train to London—yes, I would do that, spend the night there—get my ideas sorted out. And then I remembered that I couldn't do that. I had a guest coming to dinner.

(Leave a note on the back door, tell him you had an urgent call—anything—a dinner date, Mab Fenwick, you're out of your head—a dinner date with whom? You don't even even know his name. And, one might add, on the evidence of that portrait you've just seen—with what? An Elizabethan gentleman who died over four hundred years ago. Charming!)

At the bus station, I discovered that this wasn't my lucky day either. I had just missed the Wynsley connection and would have a two-hour wait for the next one. Of course, it was only two miles. I could walk, although my parcels were beginning to make me feel as if I had one arm longer than the other. Even as I pondered, the rain began again. That decided me, and I put the bag into left-luggage and wandered back along the main street, staring in the shop windows, looking for a pleasant restaurant where I could have fish and chips. Abchester boasted nothing so delicate as a genteel teashop or restaurant, only a noisy teenage snack-bar complete with blaring juke box and plastic tables. In desperation I went inside but the struggle to find a vacant table was too much. I gave up. I would be as well to return to the bus station with its dismal "Refreshments."

As I walked past a shop which carried a sign "Antiques," I noticed a woman putting a china ornament in the window. She looked up, saw me and waved. The smile was somewhat familiar. She came to the door and said:

"Miss Fenwick, isn't it? Sorry we got sidetracked last night. Do come in—at least until the rain has stopped. It's probably just a shower."

It was Dulcie Willis.

"Good gracious—I'm sorry, I hardly recognised you."

She laughed. "The red wig and the painted face are part of Queen Elizabeth, my dear—and a very authentic part if she is to be correctly portrayed. You must have thought I was very inexpert with my powder and paint—"

She was much prettier and considerably

164

younger than I had thought her at first meeting. A bright attractive woman in her mid-thirties, with a glossy blonde elegance better fitted to a boutique in Bond Street than "The Old Curio Shop" sandwiched between the supermarket and the bakery, its windows packed with bric-a-brac rather than the lofty antiques the sign suggested.

She saw me looking round and said: "Do feel free to wander." And as if she had read my mind, added: "I'm afraid I deal more with dusty relics from Victorian Abchester than true antiques. Of course, occasionally I am fortunate and Granny's dusty old cupboard yields a piece of Cranberry glass or a Bristol paperweight." She looked around the crowded shelves with a good-humoured shrug. "Of course, it's my own fault, really. I never could resist a good sob story and some of the old dears, desperate for cash these days—and who isn't—bring to me what they regard as their treasures, things that have been handed down to them. Worthless, of course. They don't seem to know the difference between merely old and antique. And bless their dear hearts, I have to break it to them very gently and end up paying far more for it to sit on my shelf than I'll ever recover for it in the market. Oh well, I might be old and poor myself some day."

I rather doubted that. Beneath the charm and the sweetness, I suspected a very shrewd lady held sway over the sentimental one she was telling me about. It was just a feeling, nothing I could readily qualify from my slender acquaintance and what Mrs. Timmons had told me. First impressions could be false, and often were, but I knew that in a tight corner my appeal for help would be to Mrs. Timmons, garrulous or not.

The phone rang upstairs and she excused herself. I was inspecting some rather dismal plates when she returned. "That was my uncle—Mr. Willis, the solicitor. I believe you've met—"

Strange, but I would never have connected the Dickensian gent as a blood relation, perhaps because he had been as distant as she was eager to be friendly.

She looked at one of the many dusty clocks. "D'you know, I think I'll shut up shop for a couple of hours. I don't think I'll be overburdened with customers," she added ruefully, "or miss my big sale of the week. Oh, good—the rain's stopped."

As she picked up a sign to hang on the door, I prepared to take my departure, and out of politeness felt I ought to purchase the china plate.

"I'll take this, please."

She smiled at me, took it out of my hands and said: "Don't—it isn't genuine, nor is it worth seventy-five pence. It'll be quite out of place at Wynsley." She cut short my polite protests: "Have you had any lunch? Right—come upstairs to the flat, and I'll make some coffee. You won't get much. My figure says I'm not allowed a hefty lunch—cheese and biscuits all right with you?"

I told her that it was the coffee I would most appreciate, and that I had been searching for a suitable place when she'd seen me outside.

"I'm glad I rescued you then—cafés here in Abchester are a fate worse than death. Not an experience to be undertaken lightly. Some day, if I ever strike it rich —you know, the sort of thing we antique people dream of, buying an oil painting for sixpence for the frame and having it turn out to be a Constable once the dirt is scraped off—where was I? Oh, yes, if I ever have a piece of luck like that, I'm going to open an elegant restaurant in Abchester, its first ever. Lovely dinners with candlelight and wine and—please God, for those of us not so young as we were, some subdued lighting."

The flat was pleasant, furnished with taste but disappointingly lacking in the finer touches one would expect from Dulcie Willis' professional zeal. The outlook from the window was frankly hideous, and she said so. I picked up a magazine on antiques from the coffee table as she chatted from the tiny kitchen which connected with the sitting room. It was all general conversation about the Flower Festival and how thrilled she had been at winning. She still couldn't believe it, as everyone else's floats had seemed so much prettier than hers. Finally she sat down opposite with the tray and the promised cheese and biscuits. The coffee, fresh ground and strong, was delicious. I asked what kind it was and resolved to invest in a quantity, especially for my visitor that evening.

Oh, dear God, what if he isn't *real*—I could have wept.

"Is everything all right, Miss Fenwick?" I could hear her voice a long way off.

"Yes, of course."

"Sure? For a moment, you looked quite strange."

"Did I? I was just trying to remember if I'd bought all the things I needed—stocking the refrigerator, you know—for Derek coming home again." I hadn't meant to name-drop like that, but she seized the topic eagerly.

"Aren't you a lucky girl? And so are we, for that matter—super to have the famous Derek Wynsley coming to live in this area. Aren't you absolutely thrilled at the prospect of marrying Sir Amyas Symon? I just adore his adventures. The last serial I thought was the best of the lot—trouble with most of them is that after one or two series, one begins to get bored. But each time Sir Amyas is better than the last—I hope they have a lot more lined up."

"As a matter of fact, he's working on the next series at the moment. That's why he's in Derbyshire just now. They're filming some location scenes."

"How absolutely marvellous. Oh, I shall look forward to that—lovely country. We used to go there quite a lot when we were children. More coffee?"

As I accepted gratefully, she continued: "I expect you miss him very much. It can't be much fun for you, being left on your own. I expect you just long for weekends, to be together again." Her smiling, rather intimate manner suggested that she had an idea we were already married—as my dear old aunt once put it—in every sense but the ring.

"Once we're married, we'll have plenty of time to be together." I couldn't bear to go into all the intricacies of Liz and the divorce.

"Of course," she said sympathetically. "But Wynsley's a big place to stay on one's own."

"Actually, my cousin Cora's staying with me until the wedding." I decided to steer the conversation into the safe waters of Wynsley, especially as I was curious about Alice Wynsley and Dulcie's short-lived role in her sad life. "I gather you knew my predecessor, Miss Wynsley."

She pursed pretty lips together. "Did my uncle tell you that?"

"No—Mrs. Timmons told me."

"Oh, I thought Uncle might have warned you."

"Warned me—what about?" I remembered his diffidence about letting me have Wynsley. So there had been, as I suspected at the time, a warning too.

"Well, my dear, I'm not the one to interfere—or to try to influence anyone, but I do think Uncle might have been firmer. It's not quite the place for a female to live all alone."

"Why not?"

She shrugged. "Isolated—too far from the shops—all that sort of thing," she added vaguely.

"The isolation doesn't bother me at all. After all, I'm hardly ever alone, seeing that as I told you, my cousin is living with me —and Derek will stay with us when he's free."

She smiled, a cheerful but somehow false smile. "Oh, well, nothing to worry about. You'll be quite all right."

She buttered a cracker thoughtfully and

I asked: "Wasn't Miss Wynsley all right, Miss Willis?"

The hand on the knife trembled for an instant. "Oh my dear, *please* do call me Dulcie. Miss Wynsley—what about her?"

"I just wondered about her. No one really seems to know what happened to her."

"I thought everyone knew. She fell out of the window—took a dizzy spell. She was quite old, you know—and a bit—well, odd."

"Did you ever meet the mysterious bridegroom?"

"The what?" She laughed. "Oh, that was just some of her poor demented fantasies. No one ever saw him—and she certainly had no visitors when *I* was there, not even Mrs. Timmons, who only came to clean in the mornings."

"Do you think it was an accident—or was this another in the family tradition?"

"The family tradition?"

"Yes, it seems that the Wynsleys had a remarkable facility for committing suicide by leaping out of the upstairs windows."

"Suicide!" The scarlet-tipped nails trembled for an instant. She put down her knife slowly and carefully on the plate. "You know, Mab—I *may* call you Mab? —I know remarkably little about them, really. However, you're very welcome to all that I do know—to ease your curiosity about Alice Wynsley.

"My father was doctor here at Abchester until he died six years ago and mother remarried." She darted a reproachful look at the smiling couple in a distant wartime wedding, framed on the sideboard. "Alice Wynsley was a hypochondriac, but Father knew how to deal with her. That was how I got to know her, taking prescriptions for my father. She was rather fond of him." She stopped and looked across at me very seriously. "One of these old maids who are afraid of marriage, but actually get along much better with men than women. Father had a busy time, and if she felt the slightest ache or pain she was on the phone begging him to call, and when he did, the poor man couldn't escape. She'd keep him there gossiping for hours. Not that he would have minded, for she was an interesting character, but you can appreciate, I'm sure, that one doctor and a locum is little enough for a growing practice. I helped him in the dispensary—I'd have liked to have done nursing myself.

"Alice appreciated our interest and was kind to me in return. She persuaded me to go into antiques when she knew I was keen, and even gave me a few of her treasures to sell, insisting that I keep the money from them. She was very fond of my young brother too—he's very artistic —and she still had influence in London art circles then."

"Did you ever see any of her paintings?"

I mentioned the ones in the Museum.

"Oh, those were mild—some of them were very weird indeed, especially latterly, when her eyesight wasn't as good. I don't suppose many people have heard of her these days, and I gather that although she was the friend of Spenser and Nash and Sutherland, she never quite made the grade—or fulfilled her early promise as a student in the twenties. I think she realised that fame had passed her by, and that was why she settled in Wynsley. Not only was her eyesight failing, but she had developed arthritis in her wrists and fingers. She had to abandon her rather meticulous water-colours and splash about with oils instead. She hated admitting that she was getting old and pretended that this was just a new phase—'my mature period.' However, she was very upset when nobody wanted to buy them. I think she just gave up—if the world didn't want her, she didn't want it either. You know, I imagine, how she felt about visitors and servants?"

"I gather from Mrs. Brownlee that she was barred the door."

"Yes—nice, kind woman that she is, too. Even Mrs. Timmons—she was sure that she was robbing her. Can you imagine? Why, Mrs. Timmons is one of the original salts of the earth. Anyway, Alice was always at Father to find something to stem the tide of this progressing arthritis—and a big damp house didn't help that much, I can tell you—she subscribed to *The Lancet* and every time a new drug was mentioned, she'd phone and insist that he try it on her. A lot of them were to be injected and as she wouldn't have a nurse set foot in the house in case the village thought she was in her dotage, I landed the job of going over a couple of times a week and giving her the injections. She insisted that no one be told about her 'illness,' and my father and I respected her wishes.''

She looked at me, smiling. "You're the first one I've told. Not for any reasons of secrecy, but simply that no one else has been particularly interested. Anyway, it's all past now, the poor soul that she was—it was all terribly sad. During those last weeks she got odder and odder, but at least she was never depressed—quite the opposite—full of plans for the future." She leaned across the table. "Does that answer your question, Mab?"

"You mean—whether it was suicide?"

"Yes. My father, when he signed the certificate of death, also testified at the inquest that her behaviour was no way in keeping with someone who intended taking her own life."

"Could the injections have had something to do with it? The drugs?"

"I should jolly well think not—I was meticulous about those injections," she said indignantly.

"I wasn't meaning that. I'm sure *you* were careful, but perhaps the substance had some bad effect on her, gave her dizzy spells."

Dulcie stood up, put her hands on her hips and said: "Now look here, my father was a good doctor, one of the very best. He knew what he was doing—"

(Did he, I thought? An overworked doctor with a querulous patient, always phoning, demanding his attention, his visits to Wynsley . . .)

"Did she ever have hospital tests?"

"Why?" she demanded sharply.

"Just to see if she might be allergic to the treatment."

Dulcie pursed her lips, and I added hastily: "You see, my cousin Cora is a nurse, and she says it's usual—"

"My dear Mab, your cousin might be a nurse, and I hope she's not like most of them, pretending to know better than the doctors. I can assure you, Alice Wynsley trusted my father's judgement entirely, as did all of his patients."

The reproach was clearly implied, and I was on dangerous ground. "I'm sure he was—I wasn't intending to give you the third degree about Miss Wynsley. I'm sorry—"

She put a hand on my shoulder. "And I'm sorry, too. I get a little touchy about my father. I adored him—to me he was the most wonderful man in the world."

The phone rang, and she moved over to the kitchen. "Yes? Oh, good—Did you get it, then?—oh—yes, offer them five hundred—of course we can. Right—yes, I'll be in—"

She came back looking pleased. "That was my brother. He's just had a successful visit to an auction—a country house near Cambridge." She smiled. "I'll make an antique dealer of him yet."

I decided it was time I went back to Wynsley, remembering the infrequent buses. "Of course," she said, "but it's been lovely talking to you. I have enjoyed it."

"And thank you for the lunch." As she protested, I said: "It was just what I needed. Perhaps you'd like to come and have a meal with us—I'll arrange something when Derek gets back."

She rolled her eyes heavenward. "You mean I'm actually to spend an evening with Sir Amyas Symon himself?"

I laughed. "That's the general idea.

He's really quite harmless in his domestic surroundings—he only eats people on very rare occasions."

Despite the shadow Miss Wynsley had cast over our meeting, our parting was on the best possible terms of girlish camaradie.

I caught the bus to Wynsley and walked home up the lane without further adventures. As it is a little unusual, to say the least, to have a dinner date with a ghost, I decided to let common sense prevail, and now that my visit to the Museum at Abchester was tempered by distance, I was certain that the likeness to my midnight visitor was coincidence. I consoled myself by remembering that Mrs. Timmons had hinted at plenty of throwbacks to the wicked Wynsleys in the area.

During my association with Derek, I had become expert at intimate dinner parties, and as I was a naturally good cook who regarded this function of domesticity as a creative art in itself, I was never happier than when preparing a special meal for a very special friend. As I prepared the vegetables and made the sweet, I thought with pleasure of the evening ahead—dinner with a personable and charming young man. Surely not even Derek would object to that—I hoped!

At seven o'clock, bathed, dressed and my long hair almost dry, I came downstairs and putting on a pretty apron over my hostess gown, I inspected the roast and finished off the table setting with the silver candelabra and some small delicate posies in a bowl. I knew from experience with Derek that men loath carrying on conversations interrupted by large floral creations, across which they are doomed to stare at their hostess.

At seven-thirty I remembered that the wine had to be served at room temperature. I put it in the warmest part of the kitchen and made the final sauces, the last touches of the simple but splendid meal for two. I was so completely absorbed by my task that it was with a sense of shock that I heard the orchard gate close and footsteps approaching the kitchen.

I pulled off my apron, looked at my face in the mirror, and by the time I had turned on the record player, there was a ring at the door. A bubble of sheer joy seemed to explode inside me—he had come. He *was* real. On the other side of the door, he was waiting for me, smiling. We would have a drink together—he would praise the meal—and then—oh, then—soft lights, the sweetest music—

I flew to the door—flung it open—

And there was Derek.

8

"HELLO, darling," he said, and kissed me.

When I recovered from shock, I closed the door and asked: "What on earth are you doing here?"

"I just wanted to surprise you. Dammit, girl, I've been trying to phone you every day—every time of the day—and getting no answer. Is that damned thing out of order?"

"Don't think so."

His eyebrows raised. "You must be having a jolly time then, since I went away—"

"Oh, I am," I said sarcastically.

"You can't have been at home very much—I thought you were going to be busy—where have you been?"

I started to tell him about the Flower Festival, but he wasn't listening. He looked tired and worn. A few days filming were a terrible strain, I knew that. As I talked he threw in a polite: "Oh, is that so?" and "Were they?" and poured himself a stiff whisky.

He sniffed the air. "*That* smells very good." And wandering over, he stopped by the table set for two. Oh heavens, how was I ever going to explain that away?

He swung around to face me. "Damn Cora. I wanted it to be a surprise. Trust her to sneak out and phone you. I'll wring her tiny neck, that's what."

Thank God for the absent Cora, I thought, and smiled enigmatically. I *must* see her—warn her—

"I suppose she also told you there'll be an extra guest for a bed tonight." I muttered noncommittally and busied myself at the stove. With luck on my side, and Cora's help, I might be able to talk myself out of a very embarrassing situation. Derek was apt to be crochety and irritable when he was overworked. He needed soothing down. It wasn't the time to tell him the meal was intended for a perfect stranger, whose name I didn't know.

"She told you about Tom?"

"It was rather a bad line," I lied. In for a penny, in for a pound!

"Then we'd better get it fixed," he growled. "We pay enough rent, without an inefficient telephone. You haven't taken the martini I put out for you—"

"Oh—thanks. Cheers, darling."

We clinked glasses solemnly, as if it were New Year's Eve. He patted my cheek. "Good to be home, darling. It's been a hellish few days."

"Good to have you home, darling. You still haven't told me what I've done to earn the unexpected return of the wandering boy."

"They need Tom and me at a script conference first thing tomorrow morning. He had his car too, so when I mentioned Wynsley, he said he'd give us a lift—if we'd give him a bed for the night. At that rate he'd be sure of getting us both there at nine—and have us back in Derbyshire the same day."

Suddenly he put down his glass and took me in his arms. Resting his cheek against my hair, he sighed: "It's all a load of lies, darling, almost every word of it—"

"Methought the gentleman did protest too much—"

"I need the well-scripted lie, too." He

184

held me at arm's-length. "Darling, the truth is I've been worried to death about you, left here all alone. And when I knew Tom was going to London I begged him —on the promise of a bed—to come via Wynsley."

"Where *is* Tom?"

"You haven't heard the full extent of my bribery and corruption, my dear. I twisted his arm to make him take Cora to the Wynsley Arms for a meal so that we could have the evening alone." He took a strand of my hair and pushed it back from my brow, concentrating on the action as he added casually: "Are you all right, Mab?"

"Of course I am. Why?"

"You sounded scared on the phone."

"Scared—of what?" My laugh was a little false, I thought.

"Oh, I don't know—of being alone— left with all the chores, while we disappeared into the bright lights of television."

"You now what I think of *them*. And I haven't been alone all that much."

"Oh, did Mrs. Timmons put in the promised appearance? She's a nice old bird, isn't she?"

"Very." I decided not to tell him that

his nice old bird had almost terrified the wits out of me with her nice line in horror stories.

"Met any of the other inhabitants?"

"The Vicar and his wife—the Brownlees. They lent me a family history of the Wynsleys."

"Dull stuff, was it?"

"Not altogether. Some of them were very colourful characters." I decided to spare him Hellfire Wynsley and his orgies for the moment. I could see that his mind was on food and relaxation. He had the frown of preoccupation usual after a hard day's work where things hadn't gone well, and until he unwound, he was between the two personalities, a no-man's land of being neither himself nor Sir Amyas.

"What do we eat, darling?" I told him. "My favourite—you must have been stocking up the refrigerator. Clever girl. Have we time for another drink?"

I looked at the clock. It was five minutes before eight o'clock. At any moment now my stranger might walk in—perhaps not empty-handed, either. His gallantry suggested that he would be, like Derek, a man who brought flowers and wine.

186

could hardly get him aside and pretend this was just a casual visit. I could see it clearly—the fair man with his flowers, and Derek suddenly realising that the meal was *not* intended for him. He would never forgive me. His pride would be outraged, for like all men who had been over-endowed with sex appeal, Derek was also the original male chauvinist. And to mix the metaphors a bit, he never believed that what was sauce for the goose was also sauce for the gander! He was the philanderer, the flirt—the woman in his life had to wear blinkers and must never look at another man.

For the first time I regarded him rather coldly and dispassionately, as if we had newly met. Was it only a few days ago that he had been my whole world? Wynsley had subtly changed something of the humble gratitude with which I accepted him. Other men found me attractive—I had had ample evidence of that during the evening of the Flower Festival. And then there was my stranger with his special brand of radiance. I thought of how his presence would fill this room, his passionate belief in the past restoring

Wynsley Manor to what it had once been, so that I would see it through his eyes, adding another dimension of time.

He was young, too—scarcely older than myself—a lot younger than Derek, and considerably handsomer. I looked at Derek now with the eyes of disenchantment, and saw that his looks were fading. He had harsh lines that were not there, I would have sworn, a few weeks ago. Perhaps that was due in some measure to having removed his television make-up for Sir Amyas in rather a hurry—and somewhat inexpertly, so that what remained intensified the shadows and hollows of a man's face approaching forty. His youthful bloom had gone. Liz had had the best years of his life, and I felt resentful that I, who was fifteen years his junior, was somehow expected to restore that fleeting youth to him. I felt suddenly indignant that men may with impunity and a certain feeling of triumph, even, marry women only half their age, while the world smiles on them and says "Well done," and a woman who marries a younger man is the object of her friends' grave concern that he might be after her money, while her enemies snigger and dismiss her as eccentric, a bit odd. There was Derek—when I reached thirty-five, still in my prime, he would be fifty, and judging from the way he was shaping, fighting encroaching baldness with hairpieces, an expanding waistline with crippling diets, sagging contours with exercise and—worst of all—weariness and lethargy with long, boring evenings at home.

"Penny for them, darling?" Derek was smiling. "You're looking very solemn."

"No, I'm not—I'm just wondering whether this meat is a little tough."

(OK, Mab Fenwick, not only are you uncharitable, but you are also becoming a somewhat facile liar. What's getting into you? Derek has been the light of your life since that first meeting. You've stood by him through all this miserable mess with Liz.)

The clock struck eight and, alert now, I listened for the footsteps at the door, the bell ringing, fearing not only embarrassment but that the flaming row at the end of the evening would also be the end of Derek and me.

(And will you *really* care? conscience demanded.)

Two martinis were beginning to take effect. Derek carved the roast and poured the wine while I dispensed the vegetables. To a background of Prokofiev's magical *Romeo and Juliet* music, we dined in the manner of two people who are accustomed to one another's company, not trying to impress or be clever, not even romantic any more, just comfortably companionable—as if we had been married for ten years and were celebrating some special occasion.

"This is our first real meal together in Wynsley," said Derek, and held up his glass. "Here's to the first of many," I added, feeling hypocritical.

"If anyone had told us a few weeks ago that we would have been dining in this marvellous setting—and that it was our very own—"

"If the present owner permits—"

"*When* the present owner is delighted to sell it to us," said Derek sternly.

It was an enjoyable meal and Derek unwound and I listened sympathetically as I always did to the trials and tribulations of the filming—the absurd technical hitches, the bitter feuds between members of the cast, the hundred and one things that go wrong and yet are ironed out so skilfully that the end product glides smoothly across the screen. Another triumph for Sir Amyas.

Derek lit a cigar. "No, I couldn't take another mouthful—and don't insist, please, in case I weaken, or unless you want a tubby hubby, and an unemployed one at that. I don't see Sir Amyas being offered Falstaff, somehow." He leaned over and took my hands. "Mab, do you realise that with luck we'll be married by Christmas? Isn't that a warming thought?"

"Very."

A quick, speculative glance and he continued: "Christmas here at Wynsley. Our first—that'll be something to remember—"

"Yes—wonderful." (Oh, dear, at least sound enthusiastic.) I knew he was too good an actor to be fooled by insincerity, by my laborious manner. "You were telling me about the next episode, when Amyas goes to his sister's wedding and uncovers a plot against Queen Bess."

"Yes. He hears enough to learn there will be an assassin among the wedding guests. He tried to think of ways and means to stop her coming to the wedding. And when they fail, there's the usual mad chase and swordfight with the mysterious Black Falcon at the end." He stopped and flexed his fingers, regarding them ruefully. "Honestly, Mab, I'm finding all this Fairbanks leaping up and down on tables and chairs and duelling on staircases a bit much these days. I think I'm getting too old for the job—"

Too old. Getting too old—the words hung around us, enveloping the candles and the flowers like a shroud. Too old—

Poor Derek would never have made such a humiliating admission a couple of weeks ago, I thought with renewed compassion. Yet, although I might deny it, I knew it was true. When he walked in that evening I too had realised that he had changed, grown older. I had seen him for the first time through other eyes than those of the love-struck girl he had brought here from London. Had my infatuation for a young man I had seen only a few times and spoken to once, in the orchard last night, brought about this disenchantment!

And where was he—my midnight visitor? Now that the danger of his meeting Derek was averted, I felt a gnawing anxiety, as if he might have been involved in an accident.

"You're not listening—Mab—I've lost you." Derek was leaning across the table, smiling. "You're thousands of miles away, tucked up with all your daydreams again. What is it this time?"

I looked at him, wishing I could tell him. (Tell him what? That you're half-way to being in love with—a man? No, you don't even know that he is a man—from the evidence at hand, he might well be a figment of your imagination—the ghost of the Tudor gentleman, whose picture you saw in the Art Gallery.)

"It's all this talk about getting old," I said crossly, putting the blame on him. "Hardly seems worth taking all the trouble to move down here, with one foot in the grave and the other trembling on the edge."

He laughed. "Not to worry, love, I have a good year or two left in me yet." He sighed. "But I wish I was as sure about old Amyas. The threadbare bits are beginning to show for all our popularity, and now Queen Bess wants to be written out of the script to do a season at the National Theatre." He drained his wine, twirling the empty glass in his fingers. "Y'know, Mab—I was thinking—perhaps we could do a few episodes here at Wynsley. We might be able to link it to a real piece of family history. The nearer you can get to fact with story lines, the better it comes over on the telly. What do you think—a good idea?"

"The Wynsleys were certainly interesting and eccentric—but I'm not sure that some of their adventures would do for the box. You'd better read the Vicar's book—I'll borrow it again—"

"I haven't time. I want to have something up my sleeve for the conference tomorrow, in case the whole thing falls on its face. Tell me the interesting bits, and I'll remember them."

At the end of my story, including Mrs. Timmons' unexpurgated version of Hellfire Wynsley and the sad ending of Alice

Wynsley, I said: "Is that enough? It's all I know."

"There might be something in it, but we'd have to be careful, remembering not to offend when it goes on at peak family viewing time. However, a setting here at Wynsley would be damned good publicity. 'Scenes filmed in actor's own home'—all that sort of thing." He looked thoughtful. "I wonder if we did the right thing moving down here," and cutting short my protests, he continued: "Before you fly off the handle, darling, remember I'm superstitious—all actors are. It's part of the gift, the charisma, whatever you care to call it —that extra sense some of us have, beyond the call of the script, beyond any words written down to appreciate and expand the subtleties of the character we are playing. Sometimes it includes a nose for what's lucky—and the reverse. There are people —and places—with auras of misfortune as fatal and catching as infectious diseases."

"Are you trying to tell me what Wynsley is unlucky? You should be the last one to say that, considering the good luck the name Derek Wynsley brought to poor old Bill Brown, whom no one wanted to know.

After all, you thought our discovery of the house was a marvellous coincidence—so don't blame it on me if you've changed your mind because of a bad week with the filming unit."

"It's nothing to do with that—and I wish the answer were so simple. You don't get what I'm trying to say, love, do you? That as people alter houses to their own whims, perhaps—and a big *perhaps*—houses are also capable of altering people—"

"Honestly, Derek, I've never heard such rubbish in my life. Obviously Cora has been at you with her extra-sensory perception again." And for a moment, my indignation included a large dash of jealousy for my absent cousin.

"Not at all, you're quite wrong. Mind you, I must admit that with or without Cora's influence, some of it does make sense. That simple basic factor—the eternal war between good and evil. Some very famous actors have been acutely sensitive to the characters they played, so much so that they have dreaded playing certain roles which carried with them a positive miasma of evil. For instance,

Jekyll and Hyde is known to have exerted a strange influence on actors who played the part, and *Othello* too. I've talked to actors during my years in the theatre who actually believed they were being taken over—possessed, if you like."

"I think the explanation is so simple that it's completely evaded you."

"And what's that?"

"A good actor lives the role. What about the poor unfortunates who play murderers one night and saints the next? Do they land up schizophrenic? You always claim that a good actor switches off as soon as he leaves the stage."

He nodded. "Most can—and do. But there are a few more sensitive, perhaps even less well-balanced, who can be taken over by a character completely."

"More coffee?"

"Please." Relaying two spoonfuls of sugar into the cup, he said: "By the way, did you ever find out from Mrs. Timmons who that man was you saw roaming about the house?"

"Roaming about the house?"

"Well, he had no business in the house, and you said you saw him leaning out of the upstairs window, that first time we came here."

My hand trembled on the cream jug. "Mrs. Timmons didn't know anything about him."

"Perhaps he was a squatter. Have you ever seen him again?"

"Oh, yes, once or twice. He probably lives in the neighbourhood somewhere. I met him out riding the other morning when I got lost coming down from the tower on the hill up there. And last night he was at the Flower Festival."

He laughed. "I'm glad to hear that. You had me quite nervous for a while."

"Nervous?"

"Yes. Since I never saw him at all, I was beginning to wonder if he was left over from some of Wynsley's old hauntings. Old Willis didn't see him either, remember?"

"Hardly surprising—neither of you can see much without your specs," I said shortly. "Oh, he's quite real, I assure you. I've even exchanged words with him—"

"Oh—when was that?"

"Last night." I put down my cup. It was now or never. I wouldn't get a better opportunity than this. "As a matter of fact, Derek, I was going to tell you—once we'd eaten—"

But at that moment, luck or bad luck, as Derek would have termed it, took a hand in the evening's events. Outside there were voices, laughter, some giggling which I recognised as Cora's, followed by a ring at the door.

Cora stood outside with Tom, a plain young man of earnest aspect. Cora was slightly tipsy. "Hello, everyone," she said and rushed past me into the kitchen where she deposited a large newspaper parcel on the table. "Present—a present from Abchester—we were having this divine meal at the Wynsley Arms and I just said to Tom, Mab eats like a bird when she's alone, I bet she hadn't a thing to offer poor old Derek for a meal this evening while we sit here stuffing ourselves like lords at a banquet."

Tom grinned. "Then I remembered we'd seen a Fish Restaurant on the way through Abchester."

"Isn't he marvellous?" said Cora. "He's not just a pretty face." Swaying a little, she linked arms with Tom for support:

"Don't you think we've been clever—and kind—thinking about you both starving?"

"Very clever," said Derek, directing his remark to me, and adding in an icy voice: "But not so clever as Mab here who has, since we left her the other day, developed remarkable powers of telepathy—"

"Telepathy?" cooed Cora. "Fancy that, Tom." Tom beamed at her and, adjusting his glasses, peered carefully at the three of us, looking anxiously from one to the other. He was embarrassed and a bit bewildered in a situation well beyond him, which he guessed was building up to crisis level.

"Yes, my dear," said Derek to Cora. "See for yourself how clever little Mab has been. We have just consumed an exquisite meal, with all my favourite dishes, and she didn't know until I arrived on the doorstep that I was on my way home. Beat that, if you can." And picking up the newspaper parcel he said: "Anyone for fish and chips for breakfast? No takers?" Then bundling it into the trash can, he said, "Sorry, love," to Cora, and to Tom: "Now, what would you like to drink?"

While his back was turned I fled

upstairs. Cora found me in the second guest bedroom, making up a bed for Tom.

"Will someone please tell me what's going on in this house? All that baloney about ESP! Who were you expecting—I suppose it had to be a man?"

Making it sound casual, I said I'd met a man who knew something about the house as it used to be and I had invited him to dinner.

"When Derek appeared he presumed it was all for him and that you had phoned and warned me. He was really quite surprised."

"I'll bet he was. And what happened to your dinner date, anyway?"

"I don't know—he didn't show up. Perhaps the phone *is* out of order and he tried to call."

She was silent for a moment, watching me thoughtfully. "He must have been something special for you to go to all that trouble."

"Come off it, Cora—you know that cooking is one of my joys in life—I never consider the time spent in the kitchen as time wasted—"

"I think you might have some difficulty

persuading Derek that your motives were self-interest. Since you were preparing to entertain with all his favourite dishes, he can only presume, man-like that you wanted them to make the same impression on your date as they did on him at the beginning. Know something? That intimate setting of dinner for two is strictly for lovers—or would-be lovers." She came over and put her arms around me. "Come on—tell Cora about it."

"There's nothing to tell. It was all perfectly respectable—from my angle, anyway. He was interested in the house and it seemed a nice gesture to invite him for a meal—"

Cora was obviously disappointed. She waited hopefully for more information but when I went ahead with my bed-making, she sighed: "Well, I suppose there's no harm done. It could have been a lot worse if he'd turned up and you had been faced with an explanation to both of them."

"What shall I do, Cora? Any bright ideas about that?"

"If I were you I'd tell Derek the truth. He might just understand."

"Congratulations on the brightest idea

of the evening," said Derek's sarcastic voice from the door. "I assure you I wasn't eavesdropping on your girlish confidences. The door happened to be open and I was looking for Mab. I didn't hear anything that might be used in evidence, just that a bit of truth-telling might not come amiss."

"I'll just leave you to it," said Cora, with a hasty exit.

As the door closed behind her, Derek said: "Tom's keen to retire fairly soon. It's been a long hard day on him too. Let's go to your room and continue our conversation there."

He steered me across the corridor and once inside, lit a cigar and said: "All right —start talking—I'm listening."

"What do you want me to talk about, Derek?"

"I thought you knew the answer to that one. I'm vastly intrigued by the fact that I came home unexpectedly to what I consider *is* partly my house, to discover in the course of the evening that I had consumed an excellent meal which my fiancée had intended for another visitor, who providentially didn't show up." There was a slight pause. "A man, I gather."

"I was just about to tell you—just when they arrived—honestly, Derek. There was nothing in it at all—it was quite unimportant—the fellow I met at the Flower Festival. He seemed to know a lot about the house, and I thought it would be useful to talk to him."

"Useful—and pleasant, too. Knowing your taste in men, I expect he would be young and good-looking."

I was saved the necessity of answering as a tap on the door announced Cora again: "Sorry to intrude," she said embarrassedly, "but Tom seems to have mislaid the script you were discussing this morning—"

"It's in my briefcase," said Derek shortly.

"Well, may he have it? He wants to check it over now, as there won't be time tomorrow."

"Oh, damn Tom—tell him I'll be down in a moment." When the door closed, he said: "Is there anything important we have to discuss?"

"No—nothing that can't wait until later."

"There won't be a later tonight, my darling. By the time I've finished sorting things out with Tom—and we have to be up early. Don't bother to see us off the premises. We'll just creep out and not disturb you. Cora isn't coming up until later—her agent's got her an audition for Peter's new musical, did she tell you? She'll get a train from Abchester later. She thought you might enjoy her company for the day," he added, with a rather bitter laugh.

He stood up and took my hands. "Sure there's nothing you want to tell me before I go? No? Oh, well, then—"

At the door, he paused, turned and came back. "I almost forgot." Bending over his lips brushed mine, a kiss without passion, the dutiful chaste kiss of goodbye. "I do love you, Mab—you will remember that some time, won't you?"

9

EVEN in normal circumstances Derek was considerably below par regarding sweetness and patience over breakfast, so I decided that morning to leave Tom and he to make their own arrangements and make myself scarce until they had left.

I had crept into the deserted kitchen and was brewing a pot of very strong tea with which to fortify myself for the day ahead when Cora came in.

"How are you this morning, pet?"

"Awful."

"Poor old Mab." She sighed. "Oh, what tangled webs we weave—you haven't had much practice. You're practically a saint where men are concerned."

"I seem to be learning very fast. Quite candidly after last night I realise I just wasn't made for the role of femme fatale —or Mata Hari, either—"

Cora put an arm around me. "How about a good strong nurse's shoulder to

206

cry on. You'll notice I'm not wearing my 'anyone-for-the-casting-couch' gear today. All solid good clean fun at home."

I laughed. "Honestly, Cora—now you've asked for it. But I just don't know where to begin."

She leaned her elbows on the table in a listening attitude. "The beginning is always a good place. Quite frankly, I can't wait to hear about your dinner date—he must really be something for you to give him a second glance when you have Derek sealed, signed and delivered—almost! How did you meet him? What's he like? How old is he?"

"One thing at a time," I began. At the end of my story, she said:

"Sounds innocent enough—not even our old Aunt Grizel in Haltwhistle could take exception to your behaviour." She regarded me ruefully. "Thing is, of course, whether you fancy him or no. Honest now—your secret will be safe with me."

"I suppose I do—a bit."

"A bit more than Derek, for instance?"

I thought for a moment. "I don't know —I can't answer that until I've had a chance to get to know him better—sit down and really talk to him—"

"Like last night—if all had gone according to plan."

"Yes."

She whistled softly. "All that *grande passion* for Derek felled in one mighty swoop—and for a man whose name you don't even know. For the faithful, long-suffering Victorian heroine that is Derek's image of you—and mine, too, for that matter—you are really moving into the twentieth century with a bang. Keep it up, honey, and you'll be sleeping around in no time." She paused. "One more indelicate question. I suppose if your lovely stranger asked you, you *would?*"

I thought for a moment and Cora smiled: "And if you have to consider it so carefully, you would all right. Poor old Derek—I never thought a time would come when I'd really feel sorry for him!"

"Do you still feel anything about this house—you know that it's haunted?" I asked as we went upstairs.

"I haven't had time to notice it. I've been too involved with the troubles of the present inhabitants." She looked around.

frowning. "I don't like the stairs here—I do get an impression that I have to walk round someone who's meeting me, half-way up, and I wouldn't care to walk down in the middle of the night in a storm, if the bathroom was on the lower floor, for instance. Still, I also get the impression that he's a nice old fella."

I told her about Sir John, and that I was sure I had heard someone call: Mirabel. "Sir John searching for his long-lost daughter?" She laughed. "Could be—well, at least you're not in any danger. Quite honestly, pet, I think you've got noises in the ear—very common with heavy catarrhal conditions, following allergies to summer pollen. I've got just the thing for you in my little black bag." I followed her into the bedroom and she gave me some pills in a bottle. "These should do the trick."

As she packed her overnight bag, I told her the story of Hellfire Wynsley. "A rum lot," she said, "definitely not nice to be with—small wonder the place was burnt down. Best thing that could have happened to it." As we came out of the bedroom, she pointed to the Long Gallery doors. "There's another part of the house I'm not particularly keen on. However, I haven't decided whether its vibrations are from disturbed presences or just because I'm repulsed by its sheer ugliness." She listened. "Hold on? What's that?"

We both stared at the closed doors. From inside there were scrabbling sounds. I grabbed Cora's arm. "No, don't open it!"

She laughed. "Be brave, cousin. Sounds to me like a trapped bird."

As we went in, the terrible gloom of the room seemed to reach out and touch me like a living hand—a dreadful, pleading despair. For a moment it enveloped us, then we heard another noise, the fluttering of a captive bird.

The small black shape flew up from under our feet, hurling itself against the window and ricochetting against the wall.

"Close the door!" yelled Cora. "We'll never get it out, if we don't corner it here."

I did as I was told, and after another two frantic attempts at the window, it lay in a tiny crumpled heap, wings outspread.

"Is it dead?" I asked Cora.

"No—just knocked out. Silly creature! It's a young starling." She pointed to the speckled breast, the wide yellow beak. "I'll pick it up—you open the window, and we'll put it out on the balcony. It'll fly off when it recovers. Quick now—" I did as I was told, and she seized the bird and put it outside. "Little heart was beating like a sledgehammer—"

"I hope it'll be all right—oh, there it goes—" The fresh air had revived it, and it took wing and flew down to the trees and out of sight.

"What a mess it's made," said Cora. There were droppings everywhere, and sooty marks on the distempered wall—and plenty of soot around the stone fireplace.

"I'll clean it up later—we haven't got time now. That Abchester bus, like tide, waits for no man—or woman. We'll have to hurry."

There was more than an hour to wait for the Charing Cross train at Abchester. Cora expressed a great desire to see the Wynsley Collection at the Art Gallery and Museum. As we walked toward it we met Mrs. Timmons, armed with a shopping trolley.

"I'll be along to see you later, dear."
And when I asked after the new baby, she
said: "They're both fine—and he's lovely.
He's going to be right bonny, but Betty's
husband will have to take a lot of teasing
—he was right annoyed, 'cos the little lad
has the curse of the Wynsleys—must be a
throwback."

"The curse of the Wynsleys?" asked
Cora. "Sounds nasty."

"Oh, it isn't, Miss. Quite the opposite.
The Wynsley men all had that very blond
hair—relic from Saxon days, and dark
blue eyes to go with it. And babies born
hereabouts with long fair hair are reckoned
to be throwbacks to the old family. Most
times they grow out of it and turn dark or
just mousy-coloured—thank goodness!"

In the Museum I was interested to know
Cora's psychic reactions to Anne Boleyn's
glove. She looked at it silently for a while
and then moved over to the glass case.

"Didn't it say anything to you at all?" I
asked, disappointed.

She laughed. "Not a thing."

"I thought all these possessions would
be full of vibrations."

"Not museum possessions—they have

the opposite effect—they've been through too many hands, exposed to so much atmosphere that their vibrations have been used up long ago."

I took her to the *Portrait of a Tudor Gentleman*. "What do you think of him?"

She whistled. "He's what I call a dish. I'd rather like to meet him on a moonlit night."

"Cora, do you realise what you're saying?"

She dragged her eyes from the portrait. "No?"

"That's it exactly—he *is* my stranger."

"You mean he looks like *that*?"

"Exactly."

Cora said: "I must sit down." I followed her to the red plush couch facing the paintings in the centre of the room.

"I'm worried, Cora." And I told her how Derek hadn't seen him that first evening. "Look at the colouring—the Saxon hair and blue eyes—"

"What Mrs. Timmons called 'the curse of the Wynsleys'—is that what you're thinking, too?" She paused, and then said: "That night in the orchard when you talked to him—er, did he—well, did he touch you at all?"

"I thought he was going to kiss me—but all he did was look at me very intently —from arm's length away, you might say."

"You say he was wearing Tudor dress—yet you hadn't noticed him at the Flower Festival."

"I wouldn't swear he wasn't in the procession or at the Arms—"

"I think you might be right about that. After all, you were already predisposed to see him. Your senses were attuned to pick him out." She looked back at the arrogant face. "And he would certainly stand out in any crowd." She thought for a moment and continued: "When he left you—where did he go? I mean, did you actually see him walk away down the lane?"

I felt a cold shiver as I remembered. "It turned dark—all of a sudden, a wind sprang up from nowhere—he seemed to glide away on it—and when I shouted after him and asked his name, I lost his reply—couldn't hear it."

She walked back to the picture and stood looking up at it, then she went over to Alice Wynsley's paintings. "I don't think very much of these, but it's hardly a capital offence—they're not so outrageous that anyone would have pushed her out of the window." She wandered back to the Tudor gentleman.

"I don't like it, Mab—I don't like it one little bit—I have the oddest feeling that there's a link somewhere between these two. If *he* is a ghost, then I'd be willing to bet Alice Wynsley had a nodding acquaintance with him, too."

"Why on earth should you think that?"

She shrugged. "Perhaps that's what being psychic is all about—the intuitive flash. Actually, it's a lot simpler than that, pet. Consider the coincidence—she was a sane, elderly artist who fell in love with an unknown man and was apparently courted by him to the extent of a wedding being planned. But who ever saw him? From your account, nobody. And that's where you come in. Nobody but you has seen your bloke either."

I felt my scalp crawling as she dragged out all of my secret fears and clothed them in words.

"But the most sinister aspect is that the

old girl was seen *apparently* talking to herself. Yet she sounded shrewd enough at the beginning—it was staying in Wynsley Manor that had changed her personality. Now do you see the coincidence coming home to roost?"

"You mean the way I feel about Derek?"

"Precisely. Your devotion to him, some of it ill-advised and blinkered I might add, but sweet and warming just the same, has undergone the swift cold wind of change in the few days you've been at Wynsley —and particularly since this other bloke's come into your life."

I felt the coldness creeping over me as I remembered Derek's words. "People alter houses to suit their own whims; perhaps there are houses capable of altering people, too."

When I told Cora, she nodded. "I think that may well be true. We both know— and you certainly don't claim to be sensitive about atmosphere—that there are houses which it's a joy to enter—warm, welcoming, happy houses. Others so cold and repelling that despite the host's hospitality one is dying to escape, suffocating

216

in the malignant atmosphere after ten minutes."

"I've always considered it was the decor —nothing so dramatic as malign influence at work."

As we stepped out of the musty gloom of the museum into the warm sunshine of a summer afternoon and walked in the direction of the railway station, Cora said:

"There is one other possibility, you know, to which we haven't given due care and attention. If we dismiss Alice Wynsley's eccentric habit of talking to herself as the innocent pastime of many people doomed to live alone and only the villagers' interpretation of it as throwing doubts upon her sanity, then we're left with an interesting supposition."

I lost her for a moment as we waited in our patient human herd to gallop across the pedestrian crossing. At the other side, she took my arm.

"Hasn't it occurred to you that the good doctor—your friend Dulcie's dad—might in fact have been Alice's secret lover?'

That had never occurred to me. "I'm sure Dulcie didn't know, then. However, it's quite interesting, because she did stress that Alice was always phoning her father, getting him to call and keeping him gossiping for hours. She made it sound as if he was reluctant, though and that's why he sent her to do the injections."

"He could have been leading the old girl on. Was there a wife?"

"Oh, yes, but I got the feeling they weren't very happy. Dulcie adored her father, and she told me that as soon as he died her mother remarried. There was something reproachful in the way she said it—I felt she hadn't been pleased at her mother's conduct."

We had the station platform to ourselves and looked up and down the railway line as if the train might arrive and sweep past without stopping. The bell in the ticket office announced that its arrival was imminent and Cora said:

"I don't like leaving you, Mab. I wish you were coming back with me. You should have gone with Derek and Tom this morning."

"No, Cora. I need time away from Derek—it would just have forced a crisis upon us both. Perhaps time will sort it out —a day or two. Besides, facing Derek actually scares me more than Wynsley's ghosts—I hate running away. Don't you see, I've got to know the answer. If I don't find out about my unknown gentleman, it'll taunt me for the rest of my life."

"Are you absolutely sure you want to stay?"

"Positive."

"In your position, I'd be on this coming train for London—throwing myself on Derek's displeasure—if I were you, nothing would induce me to go back to Wynsley at the moment."

"But then, I'm not you, love. But thanks for the advice, all the same."

The train rushed along the rails and waited panting and impatient for the signals to change again. "Bye, Cora—and good luck with the audition."

"Take care, love." She kissed me and was gone.

I walked along the High Street back toward the bus station rather thoughtfully —I had plenty to make me that way. I was so preoccupied I didn't hear my name called the first time.

"Mab!"

It was Dulcie. I had walked straight past her shop in a complete daze.

"Mab," she said. "I've been trying to phone you, but nothing happens. I think the line must be out of order. Would you like me to report it for you? I can't think of anything worse than being stranded at Wynsley without even a telephone—"

In the light of my cousin's speculations and fears, I decided that I couldn't think of anything worse either—except—

"How are you, anyway?" asked Dulcie, beaming. She was looking very pretty and young, her hair blowing in the breeze and unconfined to the rather severe style she had worn at our earlier meeting. "Have you time for a coffee with me?"

I said I would miss the bus if I did. "Get the next one then—in fact, my brother's home at the moment. If we're very nice to him, perhaps he'll give you a run back to Wynsley."

The prospect of not having to do the journey and walk up the lane by myself into the empty house was somehow appealing. Perhaps I could persuade Dulcie's brother to come in, break the

220

awful silence that would be awaiting me —I accepted gratefully.

"He's supposed to be looking after the shop," she said as we went through and up the stairs. "I expect he's just nipped out for cigarettes to the supermarket next door. Oh, it'll be all right. I'll hear if we have any customers—the bell rings. Not that we get much custom at the moment. Money seems to be tight everywhere, doesn't it?"

I sat down as she went into the kitchen and came back with a tray and three cups. "He'll want a cup when he comes in, I expect, but we needn't wait for him." Offering me a biscuit, she said: "What I was really phoning you about was that I thought you might like tickets for our local drama group." My heart sank as she continued: "They're doing *Medea*—my brother helps a lot, we're both keen on amateur theatricals—of course, I realise that you are used to nothing but the best. However, I would like you to see our youngsters. Some of them are very talented. I was hoping," she added with a rather shy glance, "that when the famous Derek Wynsley comes to live here, he might come along one evening and give them a little chat."

I wondered if this was the reason why I was being so assiduously cultivated by Dulcie Willis. Knowing that Derek would hate me forever for committing him to an evening of earnest young would-be actors and actresses, I said I was sure he would be delighted.

"That's settled then." She took out a couple of tickets and I decided that Cora might well suffer a little too for her commitment to the stage.

"I'll have an extra one for my cousin Cora." I told Dulcie about her and she said: "Oh, what an interesting family—I'd love to meet her—perhaps she'd be interested in our little group, too. I'm sure she would have lots of marvellous hints for them, from her own experience—"

I smiled to myself. Cora's experience I doubted would be quite the right material for impressionable youngsters. Some of her stories made *my* hair stand on end.

"She'll only be here with me until the wedding—after that she goes back to London. She was seeing an agent today as a matter of fact—so she can't afford to be too far away from the West End. I've just seen her off on the train. She came down unexpectedly with Derek and his script editor last night—a very fleeting visit—"

"Oh, I am so looking forward to meeting him," she said with a fluttery sigh.

"Once the filming's finished he'll be around quite a lot. You must come and have a meal with us one evening, remember?"

"I do indeed—thank you so much—I'm—"

She stopped and listened as the shop doorbell sounded. "It's all right. It's isn't a customer. It's only Shane. I recognise his footsteps. More coffee? I'll just re-heat the pot." She opened the door and shouted: "Up here, dear—" and disappeared into the kitchen.

I picked up a magazine. There were footsteps, light and running, on the stairs. The door opened. I looked up and the magazine flew out of my hand and fell spread-eagled on the floor. I thought for a moment I was going to faint, for there, in a sparkling white shirt and black slacks, framed in the doorway, was my stranger— my midnight visitor at Wynsley.

10

"HELLO, there." He came and took my hand in his, a real flesh-and-blood male hand with a strong grip. "I'm Shane, Dulcie's brother."

Shane. Shane, he had called to me that night in the orchard. Shane, of course. Not "name."

Overjoyed to find him real, overwhelmed by his sheer physical presence, I remember almost nothing about our three-way conversation over coffee. I think he talked about antiques and the harrowing aspects of auction sales, and made us both laugh. He had an amusing, self-deprecating manner, which was utterly charming. Horses were mentioned, too— and he advised that I should go to the local races. Even if I was a poor gambler, their colourful aspects were worth the effort.

It was the radiance I remembered most, as if he brought sunshine and warmth into the dull little room. Dulcie treated him mockingly, like a clever little boy newly in from school, showing him off for my benefit, throwing in fond memories, more as mother than sister, her manner compatible with the difference in their years. She made him sound so young that I wondered if he looked older than he was, perhaps my own junior by several years. It was obvious that she had no idea of our slight acquaintance. He did not refer to it and each time I felt it might have fit naturally into the conversation—such as after our talk about the Flower Festival—I interpreted from his direction a smiling glance which nevertheless said: "Don't tell." I was quite certain he had no wish that she should know of our dinner date.

Somewhere Dulcie stopped, listened. "Damn, that's a customer." They turned brisk and businesslike and Dulcie said: "Would you be a dear and take Mab back to Wynsley, Shane? I persuaded her to stay for coffee and she's missed the bus." She said it in a wheedling tone, like a mother offering rewards to a stubborn child on condition of good behaviour. She seemed to expect him to refuse, I thought, when she added to me: "I don't drive, or I'd take you like a shot."

"I'd be delighted," said Shane, and Dulcie looked relieved. "Now, darling, don't stay all day, will you? I have a hair appointment at four." She smiled at me. "Shane adores Wynsley—it fascinates him. Even as a little boy we could never keep him away from it—he'd walk the two miles and back and never give it a thought. 'Shane's missing,' Mum would say when I came in from work—and I'd get out my bike, cycle over, and there I'd find him mooning about the orchard, or sometimes in the house itself."

Shane laughed. "In case you think it was breaking and entering—there was a very obliging lower window which lacked a catch. All the children in the district used to play 'spooks' at Wynsley."

"Shane didn't approve of that, did you, dear? Not in your special place." When he grinned sheepishly, she said, "He didn't think anyone but himself had a right to play inside Wynsley. Oh, the bloody noses I've had to bathe, the fights I've had to stop." She looked at him fondly, waiting.

He didn't rise to the bait. "Go on, you tell her—"

"No—you."

"Come on, Dulcie dear, it's your story. You're dying to give her all the scandalous details."

She smiled at me. "You see, our mother was a Wynsley—on the wrong side of the blanket. Granny was courted by Geoffrey's son, but they were very high-class, didn't consider a farmer's daughter was good enough for their boy. Old Geoffrey might have been persuaded, but his wife was very wealthy nouveau riche." The family she mentioned widened my eyes even more. "No old Wynsley Manor for her. She wanted to remain in the Castle at Hartlow, and did. That's why Geoffrey always had such a hankering, I reckoned, that he wrote the book. Anyway the son, Francis, was just a boy down from Oxford —twenty, finishing his first year, when the war broke out. He was killed in Flanders, one of the first casualties, and back in Abchester when the news came through, our Gran was very hastily married off to Grandpa Jedley. However, when our Mum was born five months later—it's all in the parish records for anyone to see—everyone knew she was Francis Wynsley's child. She looked like him, but Shane is the image of the family." She paused. "Have you seen the picture of the Tudor gentleman in the Museum, that's supposed to be Sir Robert?"

"Yes, I have." I regarded Shane with pretended new interest. "Of course, I see it now. He is very like you."

"The curse of the Wynsleys, they call it hereabouts," said Shane rather proudly.

"It's a damned shame, you know," said Dulcie. "There was no other family. Francis was the only son and Wynsley should have come to us through the female side, but because Mum was illegitimate, it went away from the district completely, and ended with Alice Wynsley."

"Dulcie feels very passionate about it," said Shane apologetically, looking at his sister's indignant face.

"And so do you, so don't pretend," she said sharply.

"There isn't anything we can do about it now—only talk," said Shane. "There never *was* anything we could do about it," he added to me, and thrusting my handbag towards me, said: "Come along, I'll see you home," in the manner of one who isn't very pleased at the turn of events, or the way a conversation has got out of hand.

I thanked Dulcie for the coffee and we parted on excellent terms, although she was a little subdued, still brooding over the old injustice.

Shane's Fiat was old and surprisingly lacking in the dash and elegance I had thought would mark out his possessions. As he negotiated the traffic out of Abchester, I thought of the sad story. I could well understand how they both felt cheated, especially in these days of social equality. The great class barriers of English society had disappeared after World War I with the huge houses and the servants. Nowadays a farmer's daughter marrying an industrialist's son would hardly merit more than a paragraph in the social column, and even if his parents secretly thought he might have done better, they would have accepted his bride as they did their lower standards of high living, lack of servants, smaller houses; perhaps not willingly, but with a sigh of inevitability—a sign of the times.

I looked at Shane. He and Dulcie would have been perfect for Wynsley Manor. It must be very frustrating for them, I thought, as the rain began. We ran into a great thundershower and the windscreen wipers could hardly cope with the torrents of water pouring down the windows. Shane drove slowly and talked about Folly, the black mare he had bought.

"She has class. She'll do well at the local race meetings, for a start—then we'll see. I'd much rather ride than drive this thing," he said.

There was a warm intimacy in our closed-off world, with its steamed windows, our arms touching.

"So I've noticed," I said. "Once I was lost coming down from the tower, saw you riding past, and although I hailed you—"

"I didn't notice anyone, but I'm like that when I'm out on Folly."

"I was sorry I had to go to the phone, just as I'd asked you in the other evening."

"Don't apologise. Phones can be tedious —and inconvenient on occasions." There was a long pause. "By the way, I'm terribly sorry about not turning up last night. I hope you hadn't gone to any trouble—expecting me, I mean. It *was* just for a drink, wasn't it?"

"Of course," I said, lying.

"I was away at an auction which went on much longer—and the things we wanted were, as always, at the end. So I had to stay or Dulcie would have been furious. Incidentally, I nipped out and tried to phone, but nothing happened."

"It seems to be out of order. Dulcie's reporting it for me. By a strange coincidence, I was having coffee with Dulcie when you phoned her."

"Were you really?" He groaned. "If only I'd known." There was a moment's pause. "However, between you and me, I do try to keep my private life to myself."

I felt rather proud that I had rightly interpreted those warning glances.

"Big sisters watching can be very wearing. They tend to be nosy and bossy about younger brothers and think, at least mine does, that she has a perfect right to tell me how I ought to live my life. In fact, sometimes I think she's so busy with my affairs that she hasn't time for any of her own."

"She's a very attractive woman." I

wanted to ask why she hadn't married, and that seemed to be the best way to phrase it.

"Isn't she just? And she doesn't look her age either. She's thirty-seven, you know, nearly ten years older than me."

"Then you're both wearing extremely well."

He grinned, pleased by the compliment. "Dulcie could have married years ago. She has loads of men friends. One bloke—a doctor—who was a locum of Dad's, has been asking her for years now. But since Dad died, she seems to have channelled all her devotion in my direction—unfortunately." He paused. "We didn't have a particularly happy home life as youngsters. Our parents led a cat-and-dog life—God knows why they stayed together, they were so miserable—and it reflected on us."

"Perhaps Dulcie's scared of marriage then."

"She's not the only one," he said bleakly.

We had reached Wynsley and the rain had lessened slightly. "You can take the short cut up the lane now—it's been cleared."

"I wouldn't risk it after all that rain. We'll just take the long way round. However, I'll need to stop for petrol."

While he was paying the attendant, another car drew up alongside and its occupants pipped the horn and waved to me. I recognised the Brownlees and rolled down the window.

"Awful weather."

"Isn't it?"

As Shane returned to the car, the Vicar gave him a curt nod and rolled up the window so sharply that it was almost impolite, and certainly cut short any possible resuming of the conversation.

When we reached the house, he stopped the car but did not switch off. "Here you are, then—safe and sound." He leaned across and opened the car door. "It sticks a bit," he said.

I looked at him, hoping he was going to make another date, but the open door was a clear indication of dismissal.

"Must go, Mirabel. Dulcie'll kill me if I make her late for her appointment."

I stepped out of the car and, leaning, out, he said: "Sorry about last night—see you around some time." My heart beating fast with disappointment out of all proportion to the occasion, I watched him reverse the car neatly, pip the horn, raise a hand in farewell, and he was gone.

I walked round to the kitchen door, upset and frustrated. If only he'd said something definite. Presumably Dulcie had told him about Derek, whose name had never been mentioned except in passing, the casual reference which needed no explanation and clearly indicated that everyone, Shane included, knew I was to marry Derek Wynsley. I told myself to be sensible. I could hardly blame him for not wishing to become involved, even if he did find me attractive—which I knew he did. No woman needs words for that, written in a man's eyes when the first glance is exchanged and before the first words are spoken.

Perhaps knowing about Derek from Dulcie had been the real reason why he hadn't come last night. The late auction had been an excuse, and that was why he hadn't wanted our date mentioned before her.

It was perfectly logical, I told myself, that he should be casual about our next

encounter and I thought of the embarrassment if we had been having dinner
together and Derek had come on the
scene. That was *awful*, even in imagination. I was also quite certain that if Shane
Willis wanted a woman, he was the kind
of man who would be ruthless about it. I
knew instinctively that I had encountered
a fighter whose methods of obtaining what
he wanted—or the woman he wanted—
would be as unprincipled as any of his
ancestors who had occupied Wynsley
Manor in the past.

I went into the library and rearranged
some of the books. I took down a paper-
back and sat there on the window seat
overlooking the orchard, and remembered
how I'd seen him there and rushed to meet
him, when Derek had phoned. I was
longing to tell Cora the new course of
events. At least I needn't ever be frightened of the house again, since I had
discovered that my strange visitor was real.
How stupid and impressionable I had
been, imagining that the house was
haunted and that I was being courted by
a demon lover. It was all too ridiculous for

words. After all, I wasn't a mad old woman like Alice Wynsley.

The storm clouds had passed over, and a great rainbow arched above a charcoal sky to the west. The great trees were silvered in sunshine and a sea-bird hovered flashing dazzling wings like an angel of light against the dark. It cried and was gone. I put down the book whose pages I was looking at but whose words were skimming across the surface of my mind, the story refusing to leave the printed page and become fused into reality.

Shane was my only reality. I longed to see him. I told myself that all I wanted was just a few shared hours, to talk, to laugh—to be together in a world that was ours without interruption. And I felt cheated as I thought of the rest of the day stretching emptily before me in this great deserted house, hours that I was doomed to spend alone.

I longed for a shoulder to cry on. I was sad and lonely. And I was also very sorry for myself. So I took what was always my best medicine for self-pity: I became very busy. In the kitchen I seized cleaning materials, hot water and detergent, and went upstairs with my bucket to the Long Gallery. Some good honest toil, cleaning up the walls and floor after that trapped starling's visit, would shake away my fantasies and restore the common sense that had deserted me.

At least I should be grateful for the morning's events. Had I not met Shane Willis, I would never have dared to come up here again on my own. Shane had laid one ghost for me. I knew now that the house wasn't haunted.

In view of Dulcie's remarks about his early days and his constant visits to Wynsley, I had felt too embarrassed when I had a chance during the car journey, to mention that I had seen him at the upstairs window that first evening. Some time when I knew him better, I guessed he would have a perfectly simple explanation. I thought fondly that the most probable was that he came here, knowing the house was empty, to roam around the rooms, indulging in the same fantasy that had occupied his early years—that he was master of Wynsley.

I put my hand on the Long Gallery

doors. Thanks to you, Shane Willis, there are no ghosts at Wynsley.

And as soon as I stepped across the threshold and into the room, *I knew that something was wrong*—

But what—and where? I looked around me. As a child I used to be very good at those pictures in comics: "How many errors can you spot?" At first glance everything appears to be normal—an ordinary room with children playing. Then you look again, and see the displaced door-knobs, clocks lacking hands, chairs without legs and the children crazily dressed, wearing odd shoes and socks.

A moment passed and the impression faded as if I had brought the present into the room and dispelled whatever lurked there with my soap and hot water—and yet, had I been a second earlier, I felt sure that the scene before me—this tarnished, ugly room, would not have been the one I encountered. It was as if the real room had hidden away from me, put on a disguise as the Prince in the legends of childhood masked his goodness and beauty in a ragged old beggar-man's disguise.

I could have turned and run from the

room, but even as the thought crossed my mind, I realised that if I lost my courage now, I might never find it again. After all, what harm could an ugly old room do to me?

I put down my bucket and began cleaning the green distempered walls. I found that removing the soot only left sparkling rings among the grime. I did the best I could with the most obvious parts and then after sweeping the floors, I went over to the cavernous fireplace.

It was so dark that I could hardly see what I was doing. However, I swept most of the debris into its interior and was about to gather the dead leaves that had also floated down through the many seasons, when there was a soft flop.

A greyish object fluttered to the ground beside me and I shot back on to my heels as it lay still. It was an indistinguishable smallish mass in the semi-darkness about the size of a seagull. I thought with horror —a dead bird. How dreadful.

I approached it with caution and saw to my relief that what I had taken as outstretched wings was just part of a news-paper that had come unwrapped. The paper was soot-blackened, and curious to know where it had come from, I went inside the fireplace and stared up the great chimney which narrowed above my head to an oblong of blue sky. There was sufficient light inside it to reveal in the gloom a small ledge just above my head. I ran my hand along it very gingerly, expecting more paper and encountering something smooth and crackling.

I ran my hands around it, then lifted it down. A small package in a polythene bag —an ordinary notebook and a collection of papers.

I carried them into the light from the window and discovered that they were a collection of accounts, and some stubs from cheque-books. I was considerably disappointed at this evidence of house-keeping activities, having expected at least some hidden treasure—perhaps even the reliquary long since vanished from the Saxon church. The newspapers had obvi-ously been pushed onto the ledge to hold the parcel of accounts in position, and the trapped bird's attempts to escape this morning had dislodged them. Presumably the draught from the door when I had come in had done the rest, drawing air down the chimney. I unfolded a piece of the newspaper to see the date. A copy of *The Times*, the date eight years old. I looked at the notebook and the other documents with more interest. The safe deposit in the chimney pointed to one person alone—Alice Wynsley—and was quite in keeping with her alleged eccentricity.

I hadn't skimmed more than a couple of pages of the notebook when I realised that it was a diary, an account of the intimate details of Alice Wynsley's love affair. Some of her expressions were cries from the heart that I understood very well.

"He says he loves me—if only I could be sure of that—sometimes I think he is cold and indifferent—Will he come tonight—he promised but he didn't arrive —I waited for him in the Long Gallery until midnight but nothing happened—if he leaves me, I cannot face the emptiness of life without him—I love him—worship him." Over and over the words: "I love him—"

The cheque-book counterfoils were all "paid to W." for sums varying from one hundred to six hundred pounds, and paid at fairly regular intervals. Love or no, this evidence pointed to Alice Wynsley's sanity, just as the crude diary pointed to no ghostly lover, but a very real flesh-and-blood one.

It could only be one man. Dr. Willis—Dulcie and Shane's father. If he had half the personality of his son then he would not have had the slightest difficulty in charming even a wily old bird like Alice Wynsley down from the trees. But considering the cheques, unless she was paying for some very expensive medical treatment without the Health Service, then it sounded suspiciously as if the good doctor was blackmailing his patient.

And of course, there had been a Mrs. Willis alive at that time, and I wondered how the doctor had got around that just cause and impediment. If Alice knew of her existence, how did she think she could persuade her lover to go through a bigamous marriage by their parish priest, the Vicar of Wynsley and Abchester?

"He loves me—tonight I am sure—he is such a wonderful lover—"

That was the only crack in her sanity so far, and suddenly I didn't want to read on.

It seemed unforgivable, reading someone else's diary, worse even than their letters. And I wondered how offspring could steel themselves to read and publish their famous parents' secret correspondence with lovers, years after their deaths, revealing all to be lucratively serialized and read by thousands in the Sunday newspapers.

I thought a bell pealed through the house. I listened—yes, the back door. Like a schoolgirl caught with some forbidden book, I felt my face grow warm, and my action was instinctive. I bundled together diary and papers and thrust them into a dark corner of the great fireplace. Then I ran downstairs hoping that my visitor might be Shane.

Instead, I found the Vicar sitting at the kitchen table laboriously writing out a note.

He looked up, smiling: "Oh, my dear, so you *are* in, after all." I explained that I had been upstairs. He pointed to a flowered biscuit tin on the table. "Margaret was doing some baking for the guide meeting and thought you might like a few goodies." When I murmured my appreciation, he said: "Just shortbread and some of her delicious scones. Do eat them while they're fresh."

I promised to do so and he put down the note he had been writing and said: "Such a pretty room, isn't it? It's beginning to look homey and lived-in again."

As he chatted, I wondered whether I ought to mention the diary I had found. Then I decided that I would investigate further before telling anyone. Perhaps I would even destroy it, so that Alice might take the identity of her secret lover to the grave with her. After all, they were both dead now.

Mr. Brownlee was asking: "And when does your fiancé return?" I told him I wasn't sure, it depended on the script conference and the filming in Derbyshire.

"They take a break whenever they can —I shall expect him when he walks through the door."

"And your cousin?"

"She was seeing an agent in London this afternoon, hoping for a small part in a new West End show that's being cast."

"Oh," said the Vicar. "Margaret gave me strict instructions that if you were to be on your own, I was to bring you back with me to the Vicarage, to have a meal with us. Nothing special you understand, just take pot-luck. You're not busy at the moment, are you?"

"Not really. Just domestic things that can wait. Thank you very much."

When I told him about the trapped starling, he was sympathetic. "I'll get a joiner who does jobs for us to put up a wire. We had to do that. Margaret had just papered the sitting room—these young birds make a terrible mess of everything."

As we walked down the lane, he asked me if I missed my home in Northumberland and if I visited my parents often.

"As often as I can—and of course I ring them each week and we have a long chat."

He nodded approvingly. "So often with young people these days, it's out of sight, out of mind too." He paused. "Your young man gets on well with them, does he?"

"Oh, very well." I didn't tell him that, devoted to each other and never having looked at another man or woman for twenty-six years, they were shattered at Derek's matrimonial entanglements and very disapproving that I was to marry a divorced man. However, at their first meeting, he so completely captivated them, that they insisted that all the faults must have been on Liz's side.

I thought of them, safe and secure and far away. "I wonder if I could ring them on your phone—and reverse the charge. Ours is out of order, it seems—and they do worry if I don't call regularly. I met Dulcie in Abchester today and she promised to inform the telephone people. Her brother Shane very kindly drove me home in that thunderstorm."

"Do you know him well?"

"Shane? No, that was the first time we had met."

Mr. Brownlee was very silent and I wondered if he disapproved of an engaged young woman being driven home by a strange young man.

"What a storm—I would have been drenched walking up from the bus."

We had reached the Vicarage and Mr. Brownlee stopped with his hand on the gate, opened his mouth as if he wanted to say something. At that moment his wife appeared, wiping her hands on a tea towel.

"Lovely to see you, my dear—and you're in splendid time."

The Vicarage steak-and-kidney pie was everything the Vicarage scones had promised it would be, a mouth-watering feast. Several times during the meal there were little silences and when I looked up I caught an interchange of glances between the Brownlees. A question was being silently asked, and they were embarrassed when it was intercepted. It could, of course, have been merely on the condition of the pastry and the tenderness of the steak, but each looked away so hastily, I had the distinct impression that the issue was of importance.

After one of these little encounters, the talk switched hurriedly to Derek, and I wondered if they were dying to know where we were getting married and whether Mr. Brownlee was putting in a bid for the church. Derek would have loved the publicity of a church wedding, but I realized that some ministers cannot marry divorced people.

"Do be persuaded to another helping of Eve's Pudding," said Mrs. Brownlee. When I refused, she said in an excessively motherly way: "I don't suppose you've eaten all day. I know young people when they live alone."

I helped her clear the table and wash the dishes. She explained that they had eaten earlier than usual, as the Vicar had evensong and she had a social with the Women's Guild. After I telephoned home and got no answer, I excused myself, seeing they were busy about their own activities.

"I think I'll walk back up the lane now. If the phone has been fixed, Derek will call. He gets worried when he doesn't get an answer."

They waved me goodbye from the front door and I walked away conscious of their watchful glances. There had been a strangely uncomfortable atmosphere about the meal despite its excellence and I had a feeling that the reason I had been invited was not quite as innocent as it seemed. I thought about those secret looks exchanged and wondered how I had offended them.

The clouds were banking high over Wynsley. The thunder had moved back and forth all day, bringing a fretful light to the tall trees and a smouldering glare to the deep valleys. I heard its warning roll and the first drops fell as I ran the last hundred yards to the house.

I found to my surprise that the kitchen door was unlocked. I could have sworn I hadn't left it that way. How careless.

I thrust open the door.

He was waiting for me.

11

HE was standing by the window with a bottle of wine and a large bunch of flowers. "Forgive me for letting myself in. I took a chance on the weather and parked the car in the lane over there. I hope it doesn't sink into the mud—it isn't inconvenient—this visit, I mean?"

"Of course not, Shane." I was overjoyed at seeing him. "The door wasn't locked?"

He smiled. "I'd like to pretend you had been careless, but in fact that old window still opens with the aid of a penknife—if you know how to handle it."

"I hope this isn't in the nature of general information for the whole district."

"I think the youngsters of my generation will have forgotten that long ago. However, you might be wise to get it fixed. It's the pantry one—through there. I wouldn't have stooped to breaking and entering, except that I was getting soaked in the rain—I've just been here a couple of minutes—"

I had a sudden thought. "Do you come here often—when there isn't a tenant?"

"Yes, I do. Sometimes the mood takes me and I just wander around. I realise it's strictly illegal, but I don't feel morally that those rules apply to me, since I'm almost a Wynsley. You're not angry, are you, Mirabel?"

"Of course not. I'm very pleased to see you. And there was no point waiting outside in the rain," I said, taking off my wet jacket and placing it over the chair. After all, he had been honest—he could have pretended I had left the door unlocked.

He looked around the kitchen. "You've made it nice and cosy—looks as if you've lived here for a long time." He put down the wine and flowers on the table. "I was hoping we might have a meal together—"

Just like a man—no warning at all, I thought, remembering the previous night and my elaborate preparations. Tonight my hair was a mess and I hadn't even had enough warning to put on some lipstick. I did so want to be pretty for him.

"I would have mentioned it earlier, but I didn't know if I'd get away. We were expecting a client, but at the last minute he phoned—they're an unreliable lot."

"I had a meal at the Vicarage, and frankly, I couldn't take another bite. However, I can easily make you bacon and eggs, something like that, if you're hungry."

"How kind," he laughed. "Actually, I had an enormous lunch. Dulcie stands over me still, just like she did when I was a kid coming in from school. Drink up your milk. Eat up your potatoes. Have some more pudding." He sounded just like Dulcie as he exclaimed in tones of mock anguish.

"What did your mother do when all this was going on?"

He frowned and I wished I hadn't asked the question, guessing that his parents weren't happily married. "Mother wasn't around all that much when I was young. She left my father for a few years, then they got together again, but she wasn't reliable as mothers go. So Dulcie really brought me up. Shall we just have the wine?" he ended abruptly.

"Some cheese and biscuits, then?"

"Nothing for me, thank you. I hope you don't mind home brew—mine is famous through Abchester—a bit lethal, mind you, not like some of the slops you get served in restaurants these days." I watched him uncork the bottle, taste it and say: "Mm—at its very best. It's good." I produced two glasses.

"Cheers—here's to us."

The wine was good and I was in the dangerous reckless mood now where I had forgotten all Derek's warnings about "whiffs from wine gums." I was quite capable of drinking too much and, with my poor capacity, living to regret it when I awoke with an outsize hangover in the morning. But morning—who cared about morning. This was tonight, and I had hours and hours to spend with Shane.

He flipped open a cigarette case. I wasn't used to cigarette cases in my generation—they belonged to my father's time. Most of my friends carried packs of cigarettes.

"Smoke?" he asked.

"No, thank you."

"You don't smoke?"

I sounded like a prude. "I do some-times, on very rare occasions. I often think it makes the wine taste better."

"It'll make this wine taste better. It's a special blend of tobacco."

"Oh, all right."

He smiled. "Don't look so doubtful. It won't make you an addict—not one smoke."

"I don't terribly enjoy them—they're rather wasted on me. It's just a social thing."

"Then please be sociable with me. A smoke helps."

He lit it for me. Odd—foreign and expensive tobacco, I thought, and accepted another glass of wine.

He regarded me seriously now. "I came here tonight for a very special reason, Mirabel."

"And what was that?"

"Do you still want to go back—to see Wynsley as it was, I mean?"

"I'm interested. Tell me about it."

He smiled. "I can do more than that. I can take you back, if you'll let me—if you'll put yourself entirely in my hands, and trust me."

I remembered that night in the orchard, when he had told me about the house and how I had seemed to see it clearly, through his eyes. "Can you really go back? Have you found a way through time?"

He stared out of the window. "It is a lot easier to escape from reality than people imagine. We're just at the beginning, the frontiers of a great new science of the mind. A hundred years from now, everyone will accept things that shock and frighten them now."

On the kitchen wall, the telephone rang. I stared at it resentfully.

"Let it ring," he said.

"No, it's probably your sister testing it for me. She promised to report the fault."

"Don't tell her I'm here," he said as I put my hand on the receiver, "or I'll get the third degree when I get home."

"It's probably Derek," I said.

"Miss Fenwick—Mab?" It was Mrs. Brownlee. "Hello, my dear—I was just testing to see if your phone was in working order again."

I thanked her for the lovely meal and she said: "Walter is just going out to the church." There was a mutter of voices. I heard her shout: "All right, dear, see you later! Hello—Mab? I think we owe you an apology."

"An apology?" I said in pretended astonishment.

"Yes, my dear—you must have thought our behaviour this evening was a little—er, strange?" When I denied it, she continued: "You're being very kind—"

Shane leaned over, held up a newspaper and mouthed: "Library." I watched him go. Man-like, he felt embarrassed at being a forced eavesdropper to a female two-way chat that might last for some time. I indicated that I wouldn't take long.

"You see," continued Mrs. Brownlee, "Walter came over to see you this afternoon for the express purpose of having a little chat. I'm afraid that he lost his nerve at the last moment—not like him at all. Vicars have to take all kinds of situations in their stride and confessions aren't limited only to the Church of Rome and High Anglicans. My husband gets dozens every week."

I wondered where all this introduction was getting us. What on earth could the woman be leading up to. "He didn't hint at—at anything—worrying us?"

"Of course not. It was just a general conversation." Completely mystified, I hoped she wasn't about to unveil some horrendous story of sad life at the Vicarage, some indiscreet goings-on, that the Vicar was an alcoholic. She sounded exactly like a woman with a frightful confession she was dying to unload onto some captive audience. In this case, the audience was myself—I could hardly escape without being rude. I heard her draw a deep breath and thought, here goes.

"I might as well tell you that Walter and I were rather disturbed to see you with— with that young man from Abchester—in his car."

I felt indignation rising. So that was it. I was in for a lecture on my morals.

"We haven't seen him around Wynsley for some time, and in all honesty, my dear, we are a little afraid of his insinuating himself into your company."

And what business is that of yours, I'd like to know, I thought angrily, longing to say the words, and heard myself saying instead: "I can assure you that, far from insinuating himself into my company, he was doing me a great favour. It was a rainy day. I had missed the bus and his sister asked him to drive me home." Of all the cheek, I thought—what a busybody—

"Please don't be angry with me, my dear. At least hear me out first." There was a slight pause as if she were searching for the right words. "He used to come to the manor when Miss Wynsley was alive," she said, and waited dramatically.

"His sister told me that Miss Wynsley took a great interest in both of them. She was very kind to them."

"She was indeed." Again the pause, then she continued: "My dear, there is something you should know." I felt furious and could hardly restrain myself from banging down the phone. For those words always presage that the "something" is going to be very unpleasant for the hearer, in particular.

"If you intend to establish friendly relations with the Willises—"

"I do indeed. I like them both very much," I said, ready to rush to their defence. "They are so very nice and kind,

I can no more imagine anything discreditable about them than I could about the Vicar and yourself." *That* should stop her in her tracks, I thought triumphantly. It seemed that I had succeeded, for she said:

"I see. Well, perhaps I had better say no more."

Now that just wasn't good enough. That wasn't playing fair at all. "Please, Mrs. Brownlee, what are you trying to tell me?"

"It concerns Alice Wynsley and her attempts to arrange a marriage. My husband's lips are sealed as the parish priest, but mine aren't—and I am quite determined that I am not going to sit by and watch events after Miss Wynsley's tragedy."

"If you are telling me that Miss Wynsley's secret lover already had a wife, I know that already."

"Then you understand that my husband could not be party to bigamy."

"I realise that. Just this afternoon I found an old diary and I realised that her lover was Dr. Willis—Dulcie's father."

"Dr. Willis?" Mrs. Brownlee laughed. "Of course it wasn't Dr. Willis, my dear. The name Alice Wynsley gave to my husband to have put on the banns was certainly not Dulcie's father. It was her brother—Shane Willis. Nothing has ever been proved, but we hold him at least morally responsible for the poor woman's death, since he was already married."

I put down the receiver. I think I must have murmured conventional excuses, but the truth was that I suddenly felt sick. Sick, remembering the contents of that diary, the revelations of an elderly spinster's passion for a boy young enough to be her grandson. If the idea of marriage between them was ludicrous, then the intimate relationship she hinted at was revolting, degenerate.

At that moment I longed to open the kitchen door and run away, never see him again. I could have wept with disappointment. All those dreams and fantasies—and Shane Willis, seducer of old women, adulterer, bigamist, was the sordid answer to them all. And I stopped short at that— Miss Wynsley, however inappropriate her attachment for Shane, had never seen him as a callow boy. She had seen him only as a dream lover. Somehow he had cast a spell of enchantment over her.

I found him in the library. He was browsing through the books and turned smiling a welcome when I came in. It was a warm comforting smile and I wanted to cry with disillusion. Our magic evening was broken, for I knew I had to ask him about Alice Wynsley, ask him and learn by some miracle that the Vicar had been wrong. There had been some ghastly mistake. Married—of course he wasn't married—

He knew there was something wrong. He came over, put down the book and laid his hands on my shoulders. I felt as if a strong current of electricity flowed through my veins, recharging my blood to fire, directed by those strong hands, whose warmth I could feel through the thin material of my blouse.

"What is it, Mirabel?" he asked gently. "Not bad news, I hope?"

I tried to smile. "Of course not."

"You're looking very solemn. Are you feeling all right?"

"Yes, of course."

"Honest?" I said yes. "I hope you didn't mind me disappearing—it's embarrassing trying to conduct a phone conversation with someone padding about in the background trying not to listen. Dulcie's always doing it and it drives me mad." I noticed that he had brought the wine bottle and our glasses through. "Another for you?" He filled it and said: "Go on, drink up—it'll make you feel better, whatever upset you." He waited a moment for me to reply, then: "Your caller did have some bad news. Something was said that has made you unhappy. I don't want to pry—if it's about your fiancé —but perhaps I can help."

I laid down my empty glass on the table. I had been thirsty and hadn't meant to down it in one gulp. My legs felt rather weak but I watched him refill the glass without protest.

"You certainly can help, Shane." My voice sounded thicker than normal. "Seeing that what I heard was about you."

"About me?" he laughed. "Now, what have I done—and to whom?"

I couldn't accuse him of seduction and attempted bigamy, just like that. I had to find words to phrase it more delicately, but the right words evaded me. "Miss Wynsley was very fond of you, wasn't she?" I sounded quite tipsy, my words ever so faintly slurred.

He looked me straight in the eye and said: "Yes, as a matter of fact, she was crazy about me. She wanted me—begged me, if you must know—to marry her." He paused. "Well, was that the news that was bothering you? Some old busybody sounding a warning bell?"

"It was Mrs. Brownlee."

"Trust Mrs. Brownlee to spring to the defence of the helpless maiden. She gets carried away with her girl guiding!"

"It wasn't such a great surprise, anyway," I said thickly. "I knew about Alice Wynsley already. As a matter of fact, I found an old diary and some papers of hers when I was cleaning in the Long Gallery this afternoon."

"A diary—papers? Are they still there?"

"Yes."

"What kind of papers?" He sounded eager.

"Old cheque-books, accounts."

"Then why don't you get them, bring them down and show them to me. Give me a chance to explain what happened, instead of listening to strangers' versions of it."

"She gave you a lot of money, didn't she?" My voice sounded slow, as if I were half-asleep.

"Yes, she did—if it's any of your business. She gave it to me of her own free will. There was no compulsion, no blackmail or extortion—if that's what you're hinting at. She insisted that she didn't need money at her age, it was no use to her, the only pleasure she could get from it was to see me in nice clothes, with a car, all the things I wanted. She decided to buy me, body and soul, own me just like Dulcie does. I was no callow boy to her, but all the world's greatest lovers—all the men she'd never had—rolled into one."

"Were you willing to accept this role in her life?" My voice was shaking.

"Yes, I was—there were extenuating circumstances—"

"Like you being already married?" Even that bombshell I had hoped for exploded quite harmlessly.

He laughed. "Married to a little scrubber at seventeen, who said I was the father of her child. Her father was prepared to make quite an issue of it, a tough factory shop steward. He could have made mincemeat of my poor father. So I agreed, we tried to keep it a secret and my father paid her handsomely to leave Abchester. I never saw her or the child again."

"Alice Wynsley didn't know."

"Of course not."

"Were you—happy, Shane?" I was trembling. The conversation wasn't going the way I had intended, for he was denying nothing. And that simple explanation I had expected—prayed for—did not exist. He was quite guilty—and worse, quite unashamed.

"I started to tell you about the extenuating circumstances for us both. If you'll pardon the indelicacy, no demands were to be made upon me unless freely given. When I got tired of her—charms—or wanted a young girl instead, I was free to go and, as she called it, 'get your lusts out of your system,' as long as I came back to her, and didn't tell her all about it next morning."

I felt sick again—the wine, the cigarette and the conversation combined.

"I can see that you think I was a scoundrel to lend myself—even as a boy—to such a despicable arrangement." When I said nothing, he added: "Like all the men Alice had ever encountered in her artist days in London, she guessed that a young man has his price—and she was willing to meet it. I was to own Wynsley Manor. In exchange for marriage she would make it over to me, and a dream for both of us would be fulfilled. It was as simple as that —marriage for her, Wynsley for me. And before you look like that, consider my background. The only son of the local doctor and his spoiled, neurotic wife. A bitter disappointment who had inherited none of my father's ideas or brains. All my life I had only one passion, one desire. And that was to own this house—I still do want it, and I will until the day I die.

"Do you really despise me for seeing the arrangement with Alice as my only chance of achieving my dream? When she was dead—and I would still be young— Wynsley would be mine. Believe me, I didn't know she was going to immediately rush down to the Vicar and put up the banns without even consulting me.

Another year and I would have been free —*was* free, as it came about—on the grounds of desertion my almost-forgotten wife divorced me.

"The news was broken to her by the Vicar—I was an intending bigamist. He told my father, who as her doctor was shocked beyond words—there was all hell to pay. Meanwhile, Alice Wynsley, believing I had betrayed her, seeing that her dream could now never come true, went back to Wynsley, locked the door and threw herself out of the Long Gallery window—aided, of course, by a few bottles of alcohol."

"In the best of Wynsley tradition," I said sarcastically and when he held out the bottle towards my glass, I put my hand over it. "No, thank you." Somehow I misjudged the distance and the glass fell to the floor and broke. My eyes pricking with tears, I bent to retrieve the pieces and discovered that I was feeling the effects of the wine. Combined with the cigarette I had smoked, I was distinctly giddy, and my eyes felt odd, too. The room had taken on a luminous quality. Instead of the empty bookshelves looking dusty, dead and deserted, the whole room seemed to be sparkling, coming alive.

Fascinated, I watched the drops of wine drip on to the floor by my chair, hearing the sound each one made, shining bright as blood.

"Darling, you're bleeding. You've cut your fingers."

He knelt down beside me, and lifting my hand gently to his lips, licked away the blood. I felt his tongue, warm and sensual on my fingers. I looked up and his face was close to mine and I slid, with a little moan of pleasure, into his waiting arms. I tasted my own blood on his lips as we kissed long and deep. The warmth and urgency of this new-born love and the need of consummation was frustrated by the chill library floor. In practical terms, I thought of the discomfort of making love there when more accommodating places awaited upstairs. I thought with longing of my four-poster bed.

As if Shane had the same thought, he drew me to my feet, whispered: "Come along, darling." He put an arm around my shoulders as he opened the door. "This is where our wonderful journey begins, my love," and together we climbed the great staircase. It also seemed to gleam and throb with light, from which all the dust, the weariness of the passing centuries had vanished. The oak was new. I could smell the sweet resin of felled trees—the plaster of the ceilings was hardly dry.

At the door of my bedroom, I paused, my hand on the latch.

"No, my dearest—not yet. Afterwards we will go there—and you will sleep in my arms all night long. There will be no barriers, we will be one flesh—one love— but first I want you to come into my magic world and see Wynsley as it once was. You still want that, don't you? Then come with me."

I went with him toward the Long Gallery. He smiled and said: "When I open these doors, we will walk into the past. If you have faith and believe in me, then the Gallery will be as it was—as it exists in your mind, as you would have it be. That I promise you." And leaning against the door, he took me into his arms again. "There is still time to say no—still time to go back. Or are you really mine now and for always, Mirabel?"

"Always." I heard my voice from far away. "Always." And when he kissed me there was so little pressure on my bruised mouth, that he seemed already a shadow within shadows.

He opened the door and I felt a sense of bitter disappointment. There was the ugly room, the green distempered wall, the windows. He walked across and opened them, stood with his back against the light and said: "Look again, Mirabel—look at the world I have brought you—"

As he spoke I was aware of daylight fading, as in the path of an oncoming storm. The room was cold—growing colder, and in the sky beyond the windows, the clouds were moving rapidly. Day was becoming night, night had changed into day, and all in the blink of an eye.

Suddenly I was blinded by moonlight which streamed through the window, casting a delicate pattern of lattice-work on the floorboards. But it was the moonlight of another age. Before my eyes, the Gallery was changing shape, growing longer, four, five times its length—the ugly distempered wall disappeared with its hateful modern window. In its place a great stained-glass arch, a Tudor window sheathed in stone. On and on the transformation continued, the room lengthening, widening, beautiful and yet more beautiful.

Now the moonlight grew stronger, touched the great carved ceiling, the panelled walls, the embrasures with more windows, the portraits gleaming in firelight. Firelight—the stone fireplace held a huge log fire which hissed and crackled. A high-backed chair stood beside it, with a footstool, and beyond, a great carved table. Shadows of other furniture gleamed now, chests and tapestries stood against the walls, sconces holding rushlights added to the moon's illumination.

And far at the other end of the gallery, he was waiting for me, his smile an invitation I could not resist. "Tonight we will be together for all eternity." I heard his voice as if he were close at my side. I began to walk across the floor, the moonlight beckoning, strewing diamonds of welcome in my path.

Suddenly from the shadows one moved, took shape and came to my side.

My lover, my lover—I thought—no

longer Shane Willis, but only his spirit released from the shell of the twentieth century, returned to the world that had created him.

"For us there will be no ending. The past is world without end. In death undefeated—" Shane Willis was Wynsley, the house and its people. He was all of them, indivisible.

"Mirabel." It was another voice, one I had heard before. "Mirabel." The shadow at my side had grown and as I looked toward the shape it formed, I felt both fear and disappointment. An elderly man in shabby eighteenth-century coat, his wig awry—"Mirabel." As he said my name I saw that his teeth were rotten, black stumps and I felt his ghastly breath on my face. Not only his breath but his whole person smelled abominable—his face and hands were filthy—

"Mirabel—" I recognised that pleasing voice and I tried to remember—where—I knew him, but as yet his name escaped me. He was from some remembered dream just beyond the edge of consciousness.

"Come—come—come to me—for us there is no ending—" The other voice interrupted, the voice of my love at the far end of the Gallery, standing by the massive window—waiting—waiting—

"No, Mirabel. No!" And as I moved forward, my arms were seized and held in a vice-like grip by the old man. "No—you must not—"

"Let me go!" I cried.

"Thrust him out of your mind—he only exists there," said the voice of my love. "Close your mind to him—walk—walk—come to me—"

"Let me *go*—"

But I couldn't escape the strong arms that imprisoned me, the nearness, the stench of his unwashed body, the stale sweat and soiled linen.

"I beseech you, Mirabel—do not—do not—"

"Walk! Walk!" the figure by the window commanded. "Come! Come to me!"

"Mirabel—I am pleading with you—"

"Mirabel, my love—my love—hurry, hurry—"

"No—not another step—not one—there is danger, Mirabel—"

At that moment, I felt the room shaking

beneath my feet and I was blinded by a light that swept across the room towards me. It grew larger, brighter—a great orb like the sun. It lit up the face of my captor, the old man who had lived and died on earth as Sir John Wynsley.

Now the light was unbearably close, making me blink. Something was happening to the room. The scene was changing, shifting, slipping out of focus like a tapestry stirred by the wind. The moonlight too was fading, the room growing lighter. There was a deep throbbing note from close at hand—a sound I should have recognised—

"You are safe now—safe, Mirabel. Your friends are here." And my captor released the vice-like grip on my shoulders. There was a smile on the tired, ugly old face. Then I heard a voice from far away call:

"Mab—for God's sake Mab—get back!"

The voice I recognised. It was from my own world, and the old man at my side, still smiling, grew transparent and vanished. And the Long Gallery with him.

I blinked and focused my eyes to find that I was standing in the cold evening air, with my feet pressed hard against the edge of the tiny balcony.

With thirty feet of empty space between me and the broken flagstones of the terrace far below.

12

"**M**AB!" Derek's face stared up at me from far below. White, strained, he begged: "Go back, Mab—now. And be careful—steady, now—"

I did as I was told and took a step backward into the room with its ugly green distempered wall, its beauty that I had witnessed so briefly returned again to the long-dead world of yesterday.

Behind me the door opened and Cora rushed in.

"Oh, Cora," I clung to her gratefully. "Where's Derek now?"

"He's gone in pursuit of your burglar." She went to the window. "Look, down there." As I went over, she said hastily, "You get away from the window—now don't worry, Derek will get him."

I could see the two men fighting, Shane and Derek, beating at each other with their fists like madmen, or like extras in a poor film. Suddenly they broke apart.

Shane clambered over the garden wall, kicking back at Derek, who tried to seize his ankles. For a moment, Derek was sprawling on the ground, then he, too, was clambering over the wall which hid them both from view.

They reappeared among the uncut grass beyond the terrace, grappling and struggling, with no holds barred. In the gathering dusk it was difficult to see who was up on his feet and who was down on the ground. Occasionally they broke loose from the flailing fists, one raced away, pursued by the other—and the fight began all over again. They were evenly matched in height and weight, and Derek's hair was only shades darker than Shane's. Soon they were both so begrimed as the gathering dusk swallowed them, that they became indistinguishable, vanishing into the overgrowth of the hedgerows.

Cora looked around the room. "Where's the other man?"

"What other man?"

"When you were struggling with your burglar, I distinctly saw a second man. Maybe it was just the fault of the shadows or something, because I thought he was wearing—don't laugh, please—I thought he was wearing eighteenth-century clothes and a wig which was in danger of coming unstuck—"

I was too concerned about Derek to launch into the part Sir John or his ghost had played in my rescue. Cora's amazing psychic powers would have to wait for a more opportune moment.

Derek and Shane did not reappear. Searching the growing darkness, I said, "We must go after them."

"You're not going anywhere, Mab. Not until Cora gets some explanations. What on earth have you been up to?" She paused. "The man who ran away—he isn't really a burglar, is he? I thought not. He looked like your handsome stranger. Right? Why was he trying to push you out of the window?"

"I'll tell you later. Oh, where *is* Derek?"

Cora peered out of the window. "Can't see either of them now, can you? Incidentally, you'd better be thinking up a good story, my pet. I don't know what kind of a party you've been at—or where you got the stuff—but you're as high as a kite—drugged to the eyeballs."

I followed her to the door. I had to find Shane—know the truth—

"Come on, sweetie-pie, Cora will make you a nice big cup of black coffee, frighten away the grues. Derek'll have a fit if he sees you in this condition. He's very stern and old-fashioned about drug-taking, you know."

I had an idea of how to get rid of her. "Cora, wait a minute—I found a diary when I was cleaning up after the starling here this afternoon—"

"Whose diary?"

"Alice Wynsley's, of course. It's over there by the fireplace—"

"Hold on, I'll get it."

As she left my side, I slipped out of the door and locked it behind me. Her indignant cries, demanding to be freed and calling me all the insulting names she could think of, were the last thing I heard as I rushed downstairs and out into the night.

I followed the path where I had seen the two men disappear, and by the time I had raced around the corner where the lane leads down to the Vicarge, I was just in time to see the Porsche Carrera drive off.

"Derek—Derek," I called. "Wait—wait—"

He never heard me, accelerating madly, and at that moment I saw what he intended to do. There was his quarry, a distant figure rushing through the old graveyard, where I had lost my way a few days earlier. I watched the fast disappearing car. By racing around two sides of the triangle formed by lane and graveyard, Derek was going to head him off before he reached the main Abchester road.

I stood there for a moment, wondering what to do next, my fuddled brain insisting on the necessity of explanation. I had to explain to someone, sort things out between the two men before they did further damage to one another. I was convinced the whole thing was my fault. Perhaps I could talk to them, put everything right—perhaps the most plausible explanation would occur to me before their inevitable meeting and the fighting between them was resumed.

"Shane—Shane!" I called. I didn't really expect any reply, and I ran through the wilderness of overgrown grass until I reached the barbed wire fence. Scrambling underneath I found myself once more in the old graveyard. By day it was hardly an inspiring sight, but in the gloaming, with shadows growing from every corner, it was not a place for the faint-hearted, and I fully understood the reputation it had acquired for being haunted.

"Shane." There was no answer, only the grass moving, which might have been the breeze. The tombstones with their leering angels, their lichened skulls-and-cross-bones, peering above the long grass, suggested that someone might be waiting behind them, crouched in ambush, ready to seize me as I slipped past. I thought of ghostly hands stretching out.

"Shane, are you there?" My voice was trembling, for only the flattened grass indicated that someone human had gone this way before me. Even the unsteady tracks were becoming harder to follow as the light faded. Beyond the graveyard the evening gloom was penetrated by the first orange lamps glowing in neat lines along the motorway and on the Abchester road.

Occasionally I stopped to listen, feeling

frightened and alone, steeling myself not to remember where I was or to imagine the long-dead inhabitants whose dust lay in neat, regulated patterns below the turmoil of weeds.

"Shane?" Why had he deserted me when I had so many questions to ask? "Shane?" But it was only the tall grass moving.

Suddenly the silence around me was shattered by another sound—a car—the Porsche, hammering down the Vicarage lane only thirty yards away from me. There were glimpses of it speeding past, through the hedgerow. I waved my arms, running toward it, shouting: "Derek— here—Derek!"

I was glad he was wasting his time, that Shane had escaped. Perhaps if I drew his attention, I could delay matters further.

At that moment the night was shattered by the hideous screech of brakes. The Porsche had reached the main road. There was the grinding, sickening sound of tearing metal—and silence. I began to run in the direction of the sound, the scene hidden from me by the hedgerow.

And the silence was ripped apart by a

great explosion which shook the earth beneath my feet, the evening sky illuminated by great flames licking the edges of the field.

"Derek!" I screamed. I reached the gate, climbed over, but by the time I was twenty feet away from the blazing car, I knew there was nothing I nor anyone else could do to save him. For a moment against the ghastly red light of burning petrol I saw a dark figure slumped over the wheel. Even as I looked it slipped sideways, vanished into the inferno.

"Oh God—Oh God," I wept as the last adventure of Sir Amyas Symon came to its bitter and terrible end. I dropped to my knees and cried, leaning my head on the grass verge, sick, wishing I could die, too.

The sickness had taken away some of the drug effects with it. The road was full of voices. People were everywhere.

"There's another of them—a woman up here." Someone rushed up to me and said: "Were you in the car too? Were you thrown clear? Or did it knock you down? Are you badly hurt? No, no—stay where you are—don't try to answer, we'll get you to hospital. The ambulance will be here soon. Try to keep calm."

The woman rushed away, shouting for blankets. As soon as she was safely out of sight, I slipped back into the graveyard. I only wanted to escape from the nightmare —I didn't want to be there when the burned-out car revealed its unrecognisable driver. I could also hear his mocking voice saying: "Great publicity, though—"

"Oh, Derek, Derek—what did I do?" And once more I began to cry. I had, through my insane infatuation for Shane Willis, involved Derek in a rescue that had ended with his death. For some evil purpose of his own, Shane had drugged me so that I would see the past—or imagine I was doing so. Did he intend my death, so that I should walk right out of the window of the Long Gallery in a state part hypnotism, part hallucination, brought about by a high dose of drugs? Was that the way Alice Wynsley had gone —and was that why he had been so keen to get her diary? What was his motive— was it his fanatical hatred of anyone else but himself owning Wynsley Manor, hatred that became an intrusion upon his sanity—the incipient madness that tainted all of them?

I knew now, almost too late, of the evil that still lurked in the house, of the influence it could exert over people who lived there. As if from the dust of the centuries Hellfire Wynsley could reach out and touch me, taking on the shape of a young and handsome man from my own time. But even Hellfire Wynsley didn't begin it all. Perhaps the one whose debt was still unpaid remained Sir Robert who four centuries ago had killed a priest to "borrow" the Priory's sacred reliquary, taking it to his King imagining the favours it would bring him, should that tiny fragment of the Cross from Calvary have divine powers and pretty Queen Jane Seymour be restored to her lusty husband, her baby son.

I was paying the price of meddlers, and I had escaped with my life, but at the cost of Derek's. I would face the future without my love, knowing I had thrown away our happiness for an illusion. Derek had tried to tell me, tried to warn me, to reach out through the briars I had built about enchanted Wynsley. Loving had given him an intuition that he was losing me, and without knowing the name of his rival, he had tried on that last visit to save me from Wynsley, from the unknown Shane and the evil that he brought into my life.

And now Derek was dead—he too was part of the past. I would never see him again, never laugh with him, never feel joy in his presence.

Oh, Derek—Derek—what *have* I done?

Ahead of me the house settled down into the night. The house I had thought so beautiful, a cold mockery in stone, whose ghostly inhabitants had claimed another victim. At that moment I remembered Cora, locked in the Long Gallery.

Poor Cora—she would be frantic. And she would have to be told about Derek, too. I felt the tears gushing out of my eyes, blinding me as I ran through the weeds. I heard my sobbing breath.

And somewhere near at hand, someone groaned. I thought I heard a voice from one of the graves.

Oh, dear God, I prayed, please not another ghost—not another.

The grasses stirred and a hand reached out, clawlike, groping at my feet. I leaped back screaming. A wrist appeared, the hand moved round carefully touching the edges, feeling. I tried to step aside, jump clear, but I stumbled and fell to my knees. I felt my ankle seized in a vice-like grip. I struggled, fought to escape. I kicked out and, free, scrambled to my feet. The old gravestone, lichen-covered, leaned drunkenly toward me—I tried to grasp it for support. I heard the moaning voice from within the grass-covered grave and jumped clear.

Only I didn't make it—I found myself stumbling backward—falling, falling. I touched something that moved—a human body, and one that was still warm.

I began to scream as hands reached out for me.

"Welcome to the tomb, love. Room for one more. I thought you'd never come." The voice continued cheerfully: "I think I've broken my leg."

"Derek!" I said, and fainted clean away.

When I came around I thought I had died and gone to heaven. There were angels floating around above my head, in long white gowns with lace like the cassocks choirboys wore on Christmas cards.

Then one of them swore and I knew I was alive, still on earth, and that the church choir had come to our rescue. Mr. Brownlee was there and said the organ had drowned out the noise of the crashing car —it was a very powerful, new church organ—and it wasn't until the explosion shook the windows that they realised something had happened. They'd all rushed down to investigate and it wasn't until some time later that they'd heard me screaming blue murder from the grave-yard.

"There are those among us," said Mr. Brownlee reproachfully, "who were not inclined to go and see what was wrong— the old graveyard does not enjoy a very promising reputation. It's the source of ghostly goings-on as far as the children are concerned. However, I convinced them the cries were human—and here we are. Margaret is binding up your young man's leg."

"What happened?"

"I'm afraid that in his flight, he ended up in one of the old graves that I warned you about on your first day here. They were vaults at one time, but so many centuries have passed that their contents have long since turned to dust and the result is that the ground above them has subsided."

I heard Cora's voice telling Mrs. Brownlee all about first aid. "Someone released your cousin. She has been locked in the Long Gallery—disgraceful business —of course, I'm not surprised at all—it's all in the Wynsley tradition, although it is a terrible tragedy that young Willis should have met such a dreadful end. His poor sister will have to be told—I'm afraid there was very little to recover after the fire brigade got here from Abchester."

"You mean it was Shane Willis in Derek's car?"

"Yes, my dear—most unfortunate. When your young man tried to intercept him, I'm afraid he turned well—rather nasty—knocked Derek out and tried to steal his car. His own Fiat was parked on the other side of the house in the lane by the orchard, but perhaps he thought the faster car was his best chance of escape at that moment. Unfortunately he came up to the main road too quickly, skidded to avoid an oncoming car—and—well, I expect you know the rest."

"Mab, darling, are you all right?" Derek hopped over on one leg.

"Careful with that ankle, Derek, until we get you to the hospital."

"Damn my ankle—come here, Mab." He took me in his arms with a great sigh. "Oh, my darling, I almost lost you—" Even with a broken ankle, he managed an embrace that the villagers and onlookers would remember long after Sir Amyas Symon was forgotten.

Cora filled in some of the details as we waited in the Casualty Department while Derek was receiving the attention of every nurse on duty—or as it seemed to us. It wasn't every day Abchester Hospital had such a notable patient.

"I didn't get my audition after all, too many applicants. And when I phoned Derek at the studio, he told me he wasn't going back to Derbyshire that evening, as Queen Bess had a throat infection. 'I'm desperate to get back to Mab, Cora—I'll pick you up in ten minutes.' We were twenty miles away when he put his foot down hard on the accelerator. I'm a some-what nervous passenger, as you know, and told him to steady on. He said: 'Just close your eyes, shut up, and if you want to do something useful, pray we're not stopped for speeding.' I asked what all the hurry was, ten minutes here or there wouldn't make any difference to the warmth of your welcome. 'Oh yes it might—I've had a terrible feeling all day that Mab is in some sort of danger.'

"When we came up the lane past the church to the back of the house, an amazing sight met our eyes. There you were, apparently being pushed out of the French window—struggling with what the police call an unknown assailant. My first thought was that you had been to a party, come back and surprised a burglar—that was Derek's idea, too—oh, here he is—"

He came out of the ward with a collection of nurses cooing over him, looking thoroughly pleased with life. "James Bond couldn't have done better," whispered Cora. Even the starchy face of Matron was wreathed in smiles. He refused a wheelchair out to the ambulance and preferred to lean on the nurses' shoulders.

They were only too delighted to oblige and went out with him giggling happily.

And there was Derek looking over his shoulder, tipping me a great wink, happy and quite unconcerned. In the ambulance going back to Wynsley, I held his hand tightly all the way.

"Poor darling." There were cuts and bruises on his face that no make-up would ever conceal. "Sir Amyas is going to be out of filming for a week or two, I'm afraid."

He grinned. "You should see the bruises that *don't* show—remind me about that later. What was he after—in the house, did you find out?"

I said I didn't know and Cora added, rather hastily: "Wasn't that a brilliant idea of Derek's to race across the graveyard and nab him before he reached the main road?"

"Just like Sir Amyas—on one of his good days," said Derek. "I didn't realise the hazards until I went down into the tomb. I suppose your burglar was the same man you saw that first night in the house."

I felt sick at the thought of Shane. "I'll tell you all about it when we get back to the house," I said. Somehow I couldn't call it home any more. Over three strong cups of coffee, prepared by Cora in the kitchen, I told them about Shane Willis, omitting only the romantic interlude in the library, which I preferred not to remember.

Derek was very understanding about the whole thing, considering. And I thought that sometimes he looked at me, rather anxiously and somewhat subdued, puzzled perhaps that there was one woman for whom he might not be one hundred percent the answer to a maiden's prayer or a television viewer's fantasy!

When the police collected the Fiat they found a vast selection of drugs hidden in it, including heroin, and I learned that Shane's magic, his reconstruction of the past, that web of enchantment too, were woven by drug addiction. They were doubtless partly responsible for Alice's passion for him and her eagerness to give him Wynsley. Remembering the strange entries in her diary, she could very well have been under the influence of drugs. I told myself that she was in all probability a willing taker, but perhaps she too had begun as I did—in all innocence—because

Shane told her it was a way to rediscover the past, and she had been curious. Curiosity which had been gratified by a walk to her death through the open window of the Long Gallery—not as she had known it—*but as it had existed four hundred years ago.*

With nothing to prove it but my own experience and intuition, I was certain that Alice Wynsley had died in the hallucination that she had returned to the past. Her diary had disappeared. The police were very interested, for Shane's traffic with drugs had begun about that time and suggested that she was providing him with sums of money for their purchase. I suspected that Shane took it with him that night when he fled in the car, and I for one was glad that the old scandal could be allowed to die with him, so that his sister Dulcie would not have to suffer any more than was absolutely necessary at losing a beloved brother.

Derek and I are married. The nest-egg which I inherited on my twenty-fifth birthday helped us to purchase a handsome, modern house on the fringes of Epping Forest. Cora visits us frequently with a bewildering succession of different boy friends. "Someday my prince will come," she says when I ask her: "Is *he* the right one this time?" I often think that her lingering glance rests on Derek, much-married, happy to be playing with our three children in the garden when he's free between series. Sir Amyas was laid to rest several years ago, his place in our lives taken by a tough detective role which Derek sighs over as: "More suitable to the mature actor."

Sometimes, when storms roll in from the west, I feel the threat of Wynsley in the air and we close the windows and tell our guests about my escape that night and how Derek arrived on the scene in the nick of time.

"A real life adventure—he outdid Sir Amyas Symon, and it's only a pity there were no television cameras there at the time."

As for Cora, she is psychic for sure. I know that now. One day when she described the second man she saw at the window, I told her that the man who restrained me from walking out of the

Long Gallery to my death was Sir John Wynsley.

"How strange," said Cora. "I wonder if it was only because your name is Mirabel, or because he wanted you to have the happy ending with your actor that his daughter didn't get with hers."

We shall never know. I made her promise to keep that piece of information to herself. I would never disillusion Derek by having him know that he was not my rescuer that night. As I've told Cora, there are some things a clever wife keeps to herself.

Soon after Shane's death, Dulcie married her faithful doctor, who had waited for her so many years. We heard from the Brownlees that there are two adopted children. Adopted by necessity or design? I have often wondered whether they recognised the danger of any further Wynsleys to follow the terrible pattern.

Wynsley Manor still stands. Its owner sold it to a huge oil company for offices. There must be little chance of Sir John's ghostly voice being heard above the din of computers, typewriters and telephones that fill its handsome rooms.

"The wicked Wynsleys have gone forever," said Derek.

But have they?

Sometimes I remember the child of Shane's brief marriage. The child who must soon be a man, and I wonder if the tainted blood stirs restlessly in him, driving him to Wynsley Manor on moonlit nights, to stare up at its windows and fill the dark house with his own mad dreams of grandeur.